DIRTY *Arrogant* BOSS

USA TODAY BESTSELLING AUTHOR

A.M. HARGROVE &

TERRI E. LAINE

DIRTY ARROGANT BOSS

A. M. HARGROVE

TERRI E. LAINE

Published By Wicked Truth Publishing, LLC

Cover Design by Najla Quamber Designs
Cover Photo by Lindee Robinson

ONE

Molly

Joe, my co-worker, had invited me to this party, which was not to be missed. It was being thrown by one of the wealthiest men in town, so I dragged my best friend Chloe along after getting approval from the host. The house was expansive and after giving it a quick once-over, I was glad Chloe had agreed to come out tonight. The mostly naked waiters dressed up in thongs were worth the trip alone. But the other hot men I'd spied so far—gah! I had to monitor my chin to make sure it remained drool-free. Thank God I'd overheard Joe discussing this party and wheedled an invitation out of him.

"Are you sure it's okay?" I'd asked.

"The more the merrier," he'd said. "Besides, wait till you see the place. You'll flip."

He'd been right. And speak of the devil...

"Molly! You made it."

I turned to see Joe standing there with a drink in his hand. "Yeah, and I'm glad I did."

"Right?"

"Yes, but you failed to mention all the hot men."

"That's because I don't look for them," he said with a huge grin on his face.

Chloe elbowed me about that time. "Oh, Joe, this is my friend, Chloe," I said.

"It's great to meet you. Molly talks about you a lot."

"I hope it's not all bad," Chloe said.

"Nope. All good. Well, you ladies enjoy yourselves tonight." He waggled his brows and sauntered off.

"Dang, this house is amazing," Chloe said. "Check that out." She pointed to a man who was surrounded by women, each of them taking turns kissing him. "Who do you suppose that is?"

"Must be the owner. Hmm. I'm going to check out that scene. Want to come?"

"Nah, I'm gonna wander around and hunt down a bar. I'll catch you in a few."

As I strolled over, I checked out the amazing artwork that hung on the walls and bumped into what I thought was another wall. Only it wasn't. It was the chest of a very tall and gorgeous man.

I lifted my head and looked up and up until my gaze landed upon a beautiful set of steel-gray eyes. They were stunning, so much so I could barely tear my gaze away from his.

"Uh, sorry about that. I wasn't watching where I was going," I said.

"It's perfectly fine. I do that a lot." His voice was deep and smooth, like velvet. No, not velvet. That was too girly. And he definitely wasn't girly.

"I can't imagine you doing that. You look more like the kind of guy who knows exactly where he's going every minute of the day."

He was dressed in tailored pants that hugged his hips and a fine shirt that he'd probably worn with a tie earlier in the day. I wouldn't have minded unbuttoning the thing to get a glimpse of what his chest looked like underneath.

"I wish," he muttered.

"What do you wish?" I was thinking maybe I could help in that department.

"Never mind. Can I get you a drink?"

"Sure."

He escorted me over to the closest bar and we both ordered a drink.

"I'm Molly, and you are?"

"Hugh. It's a pleasure meeting you, Molly."

"Likewise." I clinked his glass with mine and eyed him as I sipped my fruity concoction. "What is this?" I asked.

"It's their party cocktail."

"Any idea of what's in it?"

"Not at all, so I'd go easy on it if I were you," he suggested, sporting a sexy smirk.

"Good idea."

"Tell me about yourself, Molly."

"Molly is a bit on the boring side," I said, speaking in the third person.

He chuckled and the rich sound of his voice made my lady bits tingle. Jeez, it was only a laugh, I reminded myself.

"I'm sure you are anything but boring. Someone as beautiful as you has to lead an exciting life." He ran a finger down my arm. Not only were my lady bits tingling, my nipples were trying to shoot out of my bra too.

"Not really." Did I sound breathy, or was it just me?

"What kind of work do you do?" he asked.

"I work for a large group of attorneys. They do all kinds of legal work."

"I imagine they do, since they're attorneys." His tongue poked the inside of his cheek.

I had to laugh. "Duh. That was a giveaway, wasn't it?" What a dumbass. I wanted to palm my face.

"Yeah, I admit it was. Do you enjoy it?"

"Some days. Others, not so much. It's like anything, I suppose. It has its ups and downs."

"Are you here with anyone?" he asked.

"Actually, I am. I should probably go and catch up with her for a bit. Are you going to be around for a while?"

His eyes raked me over and a heated spark raced up and down my spine. What was it about this guy? "I will. I'm planning on making this a night to remember." His voice hummed. Was there a hidden meaning in there just for me?

"Great. Then let me go find my friend and I'll try to hook up with you in a little bit."

His eyes sparkled. Had I really just said 'hook up' with him? "Don't try, Molly. Make it happen."

Damn, that sounded like a proposition I didn't want to miss. I left Hugh, smiling, realizing my panties were wet already and he hadn't even kissed me yet. I moved through the crowd hunting for Chloe. Across the room, I spied her at another bar with a mutual friend, Jeremy. I headed over to check out what was happening between the two of them. Maybe Chloe and Jeremy were hooking up. I giggled. That would make an interesting twist. Chloe and I had joked about having a threesome with him because he was so hot.

"Hi, guys," I called out when I reached them.

"Hey, we were catching up," she said.

Jeremy leaned over and kissed my cheek. As he did, a

really hot guy approached Chloe and they started chatting. If anyone deserved attention, it was Chloe.

Jeremy excused himself as some other woman caught his eye, leaving me the third wheel as the hot guy stared at Chloe like she was a prized filly.

I headed back in the direction of where I'd left Hugh, and luckily, I found him still seated at the bar where I'd left him. He stared into his drink like he was shouldering the problems of the world.

"A penny for your thoughts," I said.

"I'm pretty sure you'd want a lot more than a penny for what's in here after listening." He tapped his temple.

"Ah, it can't be that bad."

He leaned back in his chair and crossed his arms. "It's worse, believe me. But you didn't come to this party to hear some guy complain about his issues. So let's toast to better times, shall we?" He picked up his glass and touched it to mine.

"To better times."

Our eyes connected and my stomach tightened. He was hot, there was no denying it. But it was more than that. This man had depth to him, which was weird I felt it so quickly.

I took a seat next to him, wanting to explore who this man was. "Where are you from, Hugh?"

"Here. I was born and raised in this town. What about you?"

"I'm local... well, sort of. I live in the next town over, but drive into work here every day. I'd love to live here, but can't afford it."

"How do you like where you live?"

Shrugging, I said, "I like it okay. If I didn't have my best friend, I probably wouldn't like it as much."

"I get that. It's better when you have friends and family

close by." Then he frowned. His eyes appeared pinched at the corners. I wondered what that was all about.

"What about you? Do you have family here?"

"Yes, but that's a story for another day. Would you like to dance?"

"I'd love to."

There was a large dance floor off the other room, so he walked me over and we swayed with the music. I wasn't upset when his lips sought out mine in a slow, sensual kiss. As his tongue pressed through the opening of my mouth, I thought of how it moved to the rhythm of the music. Soon, the tempo turned feverish as he sought out every secret I held.

"Come home with me tonight, Molly. Don't deny me."

I wasn't the kind of girl who easily hopped into bed with a man, but tonight was different. Things were shit in my life and this man could be the cure for the night. Plus, he was impossible to resist.

"Okay." My breath came in puffs as I tried to catch it. "But we go to my place, not yours." I might be reckless, but I wasn't crazy. It was better to be on my turf.

"Fine. Did you drive?" Hugh asked. I nodded my head. "Would you mind leaving your car and picking it up in the morning? Is that okay?"

I'd had a few drinks. It was probably for the best. "If they don't mind," I said.

"They don't. I promise."

"I need to call my friend first to let her know I'm leaving." But then my phone rang and it was Chloe. "Hey, girl, I was just getting ready to call you," I said.

Chloe asked where I was. I told her and she explained she'd met someone. She asked if I was cool if she left with him. I laughed and told her it was fine, and she had the all-clear to leave without me. Actually, I told her to get her freak on. She needed it and so did I. Then she said she was texting me a picture of the two of them.

I opened my phone at the sound of a text. It was the picture of her with Ryan, the hot guy she'd been talking to earlier. When I chuckled, Hugh asked, "Are we good?"

"Yep, all good here. My friend already left. Seems she beat me to the punch."

"Now you don't feel so bad, do you?"

"No, I don't."

He tipped my chin up and kissed me again. "I can't wait to get you into bed, Molly," he said before leading me outside.

I couldn't wait, either. This was going to be a great night after all.

TWO

Hugh

We arrived at a decent apartment building and Molly stared out of the window as if she hadn't noticed we'd arrived. Had I missed my opportunity? I could have used one of Dillon's bedrooms in his house of heathens, but he was the kind of bastard who'd have all the rooms wired for video surveillance.

Though she'd already agreed, I wanted to give her one last out so she'd have no regrets. "Should we call it a night?" I held my breath, wondering if she would say yes. Though we'd been at one of Dillon's anything-goes-including-sex parties, I would never assume that she hadn't changed her mind about taking me to her bed.

"No." She gave me a sexy smile and I took that as an invitation.

The driver opened the door and helped her out. His hands on her sparked a jealousy inside me. I wrote it off as the lust I'd held at bay since I first spotted her.

I told my driver to hang around for a little bit. If I didn't call, he could go until I texted him I was ready to leave.

We climbed the stairs to the second level and headed down a ways to her door. Her small hand shook as she opened it, and I was struck again wondering if this had been her first sex party.

Her tiny apartment was about the size of the suite of rooms I'd had at my disposal as a child growing up. My parents hadn't flaunted their wealth. Our home was modest compared to that of my cousin, who'd been the closest thing I had to a brother for a time, or grandparents, but it was still far larger than this.

Her gaze met mine for a second before darting away like a scared kitten's. From all the signals she gave, she'd seemed into me before we left. I might be ruthless when it came to business, but I wasn't a total asshole when it came to women. My parents had loved each other, unlike my cousin's parents. Their marriage had been an arrangement of sorts and they'd hated each other from the start. Dad had taught me always to treat women with respect. And I was always honest about my intentions with the women I slept with.

"Are you nervous? I know we were at a sex party, but you're free to change your mind if you don't want this," I said.

Her eyes grew large as she stared at me in horror. "No!"

I clenched my jaw. "I should go then." My dick was hard to the point of pain, but I would never force myself where I wasn't wanted.

"No." She held up her hand. "I mean, I didn't know it was a sex party."

I'd known there was something different about her. She hadn't dressed the part of a siren. The purple dress she wore clung to her like a second skin, but she'd been more covered than any woman there, including the help. "Then I really should leave."

She shook her head, the deep blonde curls bouncing. "No, I didn't know, but I did invite you over for..." Her cheeks reddened, which made her all the more alluring.

"You have to say it, love, if you want me to stay."

She lifted her chin. "I want you to fuck me."

I couldn't stop from grinning and held out a hand. "Lead the way."

We could have started there, but her couch was small, and I was a big guy. I wanted room to play. After a walk down a short hallway, we stopped at the doorframe. I braced my arm against it as she turned to face me. The room wasn't very big, much like the rest of the apartment. A bed and a small dresser took up much of the space. If I went in after her, my sheer size in the confined room might spook her. I stayed where I was.

"Strip." It was a command, and I used the voice I did at work to get things done.

Her emerald-green eyes widened a second before they heated. My little minx liked being told what to do. Not a problem. I could give her what she wanted there.

She licked her lips and went for the thin straps of her dress, slipping them off her shoulders one at a time. The little tease flicked sultry glances my way and damn if it didn't work. I gripped my dick through my pants to keep it from busting through. Her fucking bare shoulders gave me wood like no naked woman had before.

She clutched the fabric at her chest before turning around, giving me her back. Then the fabric slipped down and seemed to take an eternity to glide to the floor. *Fuck me.*

Her tight ass was better than I imagined framed by slim

hips. The strings that wrapped around her led to a center I couldn't wait to explore.

"Turn around."

My voice sounded rough and I had to swallow. She gave a coy smile over her shoulder before slowly turning to face me.

Her tits were small, high, and firm. They were perfect. My mouth watered at the thought of sucking them.

So far she'd done what I asked without speaking a word, which added to her charm. It only made me wonder at her thoughts.

"Lie on the bed and play with yourself."

She hesitated, but then gracefully did as I asked and spread her legs wide enough to use her hand between them.

Shit. I finally stepped fully into the tiny room. There wasn't anywhere for my clothes. I let my shirt fall to the floor as she worked herself into a frenzy. She was biting her lip and squirming on the mattress by the time I unzipped my fly.

"I'm going to come," she said, her voice breaking the silence.

I pulled a foil package from my pocket before letting my pants down. My cousin, Ryan, would have probably screwed her without protection just to get his hands on the family fortune. He was my competition in the sick game my grandfather had set up in his will. But I wasn't that guy. Money didn't rule my life. As much as having it over him would feed my ego, I wasn't about to take the time to talk about sexual history. I wanted to fuck her until we both couldn't move.

My gaze was fixed on that glistening spot between her legs and I gave in to the need to taste her. I kneeled at the foot of her bed and curled an arm around each leg to tug her to the edge.

Her hand was rubbing her clit frantically as she got closer. I dove in, piercing my tongue into her entrance. Damn, she was everything I'd imagined when I first laid eyes on her and more. Her back bowed and she whimpered nonsensical words. I moved her hands and repositioned my own as I licked up her slit to her swollen nub. I latched onto her clit and thrust two fingers inside her.

Her inner walls gripped my fingers, quivering as she came. I kept up my ministrations until she lay limp. Then I pulled back. "My turn."

I sounded like a bear staking his claim and maybe I was. I stood and shoved down my boxer briefs and fisted my dick in my hands. Her eyes looked like those of a deer in the middle of the road.

A smug smile curled my lips as she leaned up on her elbows. "I don't think I can get that in my mouth," she said.

"Don't worry, love. Your mouth isn't what I want to go around it. I need inside you."

I worked the condom on and moved into position. I coated my dick in her juices before pressing in just a little. She sucked in a breath and so did I. Her hole was tight from climaxing and maybe she was naturally so.

I leaned over and sucked on one of her rosy nipples. Instantly, I felt her grow wetter and her pussy gave way, letting me push in a little more.

"Ohhhh," she cried out.

What I wanted was for her to call out my name, and she would before the night was over, without my prompting.

I sucked on the opposite nipple and pinched the other between my fingers. Her hips rose and that angle gave me room to slide in deeper.

She panted and a hint of pain furrowed her brow. I backed off some and went for her mouth. I wasn't the kissing type, usually only during foreplay. It was an intimate thing, and I didn't want my partners to mistake this for more than a quick fuck. But I wanted to kiss Molly.

I growled before biting her lip and claiming her mouth like I had a right to. I slid one hand between her legs to stoke the fire there. I fucked her mouth with my tongue; I inched my way in and out between her legs. She squirmed but took it until I was finally seated as deep as I could go inside her. When I pulled back, the creases on her face had smoothed out in pleasure.

Her fingernails scored my scalp as she kissed me back in rhythm with her rocking hips.

"Damn, you're tight." I growled the words.

She was lost and didn't respond to that. Instead, she said, "Faster."

My girl was close, and I aimed to please. I pushed up with one arm so I could watch as I brought her to the edge. I pumped with a frantic tempo, knowing I wouldn't be able to last, and we had all night.

An image of her belly rounded with my child filled my head, hardening my dick further, surprising me. Normally, thoughts of knocking a woman up sent my dick to hide in my pants. Not this time. The idea of her breasts swelling because she carried my baby had me shooting off.

"I'm going to come," she said breathily.

Her words and the fisting of her walls around my cock broke my rhythm as I plunged in faster as I came harder than I had my entire life. Spent, I fell atop her until I rolled, taking her with me.

I pulled her further on the bed, tucking her into the

crook of my arm. I closed my eyes for a second, giving her a chance to rest before round two.

"Are you going to stay?" she asked.

I grinned down at her. "Love, I'm not done with you yet."

And I wasn't. We fucked a few more times before finally giving in to sleep. When I woke, the sun was high. We were on our sides, her back to my chest. My arm was draped around her. I moved to get out of bed quietly, so she didn't stir. I could leave, but something about the way she'd asked if I was going to stay made me not want to pull a dick move and duck out, or so I told myself.

Instead, after a long piss, I pulled on my briefs and went to her kitchen to hunt for food. On the counter was a stack of papers. I wouldn't have pried, but the big red stamps of 'past due' and 'final notice' caught my attention. I lifted that one and the stack was full of them.

The accusing eyes of my minx burned me.

"Sorry, I didn't mean to intrude," I said, setting the bill down.

"You should leave." Her voice was cold, and I knew I'd fucked up.

I held up a hand. "Wait. Hear me out. I think we could help each other."

She tilted her head.

I went on. "I know I shouldn't have looked, but the stack was hard to miss." Her lips thinned. "I could pay these bills for you and give you some money on top of that if you could do something in return for me."

Her words were clipped when she spoke. "And what is that?"

She didn't sound receptive to what I was about to say,

and my suggestion would probably earn me a slammed door in my face. "I would take care of you even after—"

"After what?"

"You give me an heir," I said. Her jaw dropped. "Don't answer now. Think about it. I need an heir to claim my inheritance. You need your bills paid. It's a win-win and for us both. You and the child would never want for anything. I swear."

I headed to her room so she could think about it, then contacted my driver before getting dressed. When I left the room, she was still standing there with a sheet wrapped around her.

"What about the child?" she asked.

I hadn't thought that far. I'd given up on the idea of having an heir when my admin had made demands of me after I'd slept with her. I'd thought she was a possibility. Instead, she'd turned out to be another gold-digging crazy woman. "Joint custody."

Surprising me, Molly asked, "When do I have to let you know?"

"Soon," I said. I pulled a card from my wallet and set it on her counter. She could do her own research and find out that I could back up my claims. I wanted to kiss her but didn't dare. "My driver will return and take you to pick up your car."

"No need," she said.

"Still, I insist. I would have you go with me now except I don't think you want to be around me right now."

Then I walked out the door, wondering if I would hear from her again.

THREE

Molly

Hugh walked out, leaving me to my turbulent thoughts. His offer was entirely too tempting. If he only knew the real reasons behind my overdue bills, he'd probably rescind his offer and hightail it out of my life. I picked up the stack and flipped through them one by one, cringing. It wasn't long before I was sobbing. It had been so wonderful to escape for a few hours and enjoy the pleasures of the hot Hugh for a night. Why had he had to ruin it?

Maybe I needed to change my thought process. Maybe he hadn't ruined it at all. Maybe he'd presented an opportunity of a lifetime. But should I tell him the real reason behind my God-awful debt? What if I did and it sent him running like his boxers were on fire? He was obviously from an affluent family. If they ever found out about my father, they might disown him. Or the child would most likely be disinherited. Who wanted a prison inmate as a blood relation?

Oh, good Lord, what should I do? Daddy hadn't committed the crime he'd been accused of. I knew he hadn't. He'd been framed, which was why I was spending all my money trying to get him out of there.

And then there was Mom. Her nursing home bills were astronomical. I'd sold her house and until all the money from that ran out, I couldn't get her on government assistance. Life was so unfair. Why had that horrible accident happened? She'd been so smart and vivacious. And then she'd had that seizure while she'd been driving, which had caused her to hit that stupid tree. Now her brain damage was so severe, the doctors said she would never recover. And she was only forty-eight years old. Every time I went to visit her, I broke down and cried. It was like visiting an adult baby.

Between Daddy's legal fees and Mom's medical bills, I wasn't left with much to live on. If what Hugh offered was legit, it could be a way for me to get ahead in life. But who was I kidding? It would saddle me with a baby. And babies grew up to be kids. I would be tied down for life. Was I really ready for that kind of commitment?

Then the thought of snuggling a tiny bundle of joy nailed me in the heart and my maternal instincts flared to life. I'd never thought about it before, because frankly, I hadn't had the time. Only now, with this idea planted in my brain, it began to take root. I could totally see myself pushing around a baby in a stroller, taking her to see her grandmother. Maybe it would bring a spark of light to my mom's lifeless eyes again.

For the next two days, all I could think of was Hugh and his offer, though I hadn't glanced at the card he left me, hoping to avoid the temptation to call him. I even imagined I heard a baby crying during one of those nights. I woke up and ran into my living room, checking to see where the sound came from. When I climbed back into my empty bed, the loneliness hit. And not just because Hugh wasn't there. It was because there wasn't a baby in the house. I was totally losing it. What the hell was wrong with me? I needed to see a shrink. The last thing I needed was a baby. I could barely take care of myself, along with everyone else on my plate.

When Chloe called, I kept all my feelings bottled up and brought up false cheer. "Hey, chickypoo, what's going on? I got your text, but then I didn't hear back. Tell me about this man you met."

She groaned and I knew it wasn't good news. "Ryan Witmore is a complete asshole, just like my jerkface boss, Hugh Hampton, the king of dickwads. Anyway, did you meet anyone?"

This was where I should have come clean. Instead, I said, "Uh, er—no one important. Tell me what happened."

She told a tale that left me blinking. Chloe had had a one-nighter. No, actually, it was a one-weekender. He'd offered her a job after promising she could quit. There had to be more to the story, but I didn't ask. I felt bad for keeping my secrets from her.

"And I'm currently drowning my anger in a large glass of vino," she finished.

"Hmm. Looks like you've been on one wild rollercoaster ride."

"You know it," she said.

Though I didn't want to tell her my tale, she was my best friend, and I would be there for her. "Want some sorrow-drowning company?"

"Molly, normally I would say yeah, but not tonight. I just want to hang and feel sorry for my own stupid butt for believing such bull. You know what I'm saying?"

I felt bad for being happy she didn't want company. "I do. If you change your mind, you know where to find me. Oh, you never said if you liked the job though."

"It has potential. It's not true copy-editing, but it pays a hell of a lot better."

"Well, at least you have that."

"Truth."

The next day at work, my mind was all over the place. The offer was so outlandish, I hadn't even called Chloe to tell her. She didn't know how deep in debt I was. She would never understand why I was even considering his offer.

"Hey, Molly. Did you know you missed the meeting this morning?" Joe asked.

Shit! "Yeah, I, uh, was under the weather and didn't even think I was going to make it in. But I'm feeling much better."

"Glad to hear it."

"What did I miss?" I asked.

"We went over some things on the Martin case. I can bring you up to speed later," Joe offered.

"Okay, thanks."

He leaned against my desk and asked, "Hey, that was some party the other night, huh?"

"Uh, I'll say. That house was unreal."

"Told you. I'll let you know when Dillon has another one. Did you...?" He circled his finger in the air.

"Did I what?"

"You know. Hook up with anyone there?"

"None of your business. And I can't believe you didn't tell me it was a sex party," I said, maybe a little too loud. I looked around to see if I'd been overheard.

He laughed. "Oh, that. Tiny detail."

"That was not a tiny detail, Joe."

"So? Where'd you go? I lost track of you."

"I sort of met someone."

"Ah. I see." He straightened up and walked away, chuckling some more.

He didn't see it at all. If he only knew.

The rest of the day my head was still in the baby cloud. Around five, my phone dinged with a text. When I looked at it, I almost dropped the thing like it was a thousand degrees. It was from Hugh.

Any chance you're free around 7? I'd like an opportunity to persuade you to accept my offer if you're willing.

Holy shit!

I must've been sex-drunk because I didn't even remember giving the man my phone number. What the heck was I going to tell him? One thing was for sure. I had to give him the down-low on my parents. The worst thing that could happen was he would find out about them *after* I got knocked up and then where would that leave me? In a complete disaster, that was where. I would be up to my eyeballs in debt with a baby on the way. There was no way I could ever do that to a kid.

I shot him a text back.

I'm free around 7 and I'll be home. See you then.

At six-thirty, I started pacing. By six forty-five, I had to restrain myself from jogging around my tiny apartment. By the time the knock came on my door, my heart was jumping out of my chest.

I opened the door and grabbed his arm, practically yanking him inside. "Sit down."

"Are you okay?" he asked.

"I'm not sure. But you need to sit down." I clasped my hands together just so I wouldn't rub them up and down my legs. They were dripping with sweat.

"You don't look okay. Maybe you need a drink."

"Uh, yeah. A drink." I went into the kitchen and poured us both large glasses of Jack. My hand trembled as I handed him his.

"What is this?" he asked.

"Jack." I took a huge gulp of mine and then coughed as I choked on the burn. I ran my hand across my mouth afterward. It was obvious whiskey wasn't my beverage of choice.

"I was thinking more about water. You should take it easy on this stuff."

"Yeah, sure. So lay it on me," I said.

"Excuse me?"

"You know. Your offer."

He squinted at me for a moment. Then took another sip of his drink. He was much smarter with the beverage than me. "As I mentioned, I am in need of an heir and..." He stopped and scratched his temple. "You know, maybe this isn't such a good idea."

"Why not?" I took another slug of my drink and sputtered.

"Do you have a drinking problem?" he asked.

"Who, me? Are you serious?"

"Yes, I'm serious. Look at that glass of yours. It's almost empty. And you're sweating. Are you going through withdrawals?"

I fish-mouthed, and then bent over at the waist in laughter. When I was finally able to get a lungful of air, I said, "I hate this stuff. That's why I'm coughing with every swallow."

"Why are you guzzling it then?"

"Because I'm nervous!" I shouted.

"Why?"

"Jesus. We're talking about me being a sperm receptacle, that's why! And add to that, a baby comes along with it, which happens to be quite a long commitment. Have you even given any thought to that?" Men are such idiots.

I hadn't meant to say the last part aloud, but I guess I did, because his response told me so.

"Yes, I have given a great deal of thought to that, and for your information, not all men are idiots. I have a very decent plan outlined here, if you will only stop gulping the damn liquor long enough for me to explain it to you."

"I can do that, but how will we go about getting pregnant? Will it be the natural way?"

He didn't give me any time to ponder my questions because he stood up in front of me and, before I could say another word, his mouth crashed down on mine and stole the remainder of my thoughts away.

FOUR

Hugh

The zipper was a problem, and I tore at the one on her dress, needing to get to her skin, leaving the garment in rags. I lowered it past her breasts and had to stop. "Fuck, your tits are perfect."

My mouth watered as I flicked the snap at the front of her bra. They spilled out into my hands as she worked the bra off her arms. I dipped my head, unable to resist the rosy buds, and sucked them one at a time.

Then I got to my knees. My hands slid around the back to the zipper and drew it down the rest of the way. The fabric pooled at her feet, leaving her covered in a small triangle of lacy fabric.

I leaned forward, inhaling her scent, and licked the fabric, taking in only hints of the silky skin underneath. It frustrated me, so I reached up and ripped at the string that held it all together. It didn't make a sound as it snapped and fell to the floor with her dress.

Her quick intake of breath was sexy as hell and I went for what I wanted. "I need your pussy in my mouth," I said. "Spread your legs and spread them wide."

She tried and I helped by hiking one leg over my shoulder as her back hit the wall and then the other until she was riding my face. I squeezed her ass while I sucked her clit, only to then let my tongue glide down her slit and probe at her hole, while my finger found the puckered one and played.

"Jesus fuck, you taste good." I worked a finger in her ass while my tongue fucked her pussy. Her nails scraped my scalp as she found a fistful of my hair to hang onto.

Then she was coming.

"Ride it, baby, 'cause I'm about to ride you hard." I used one hand to free my cock from the painful confines of my Gucci slacks as she continued to come like there was no end.

When she slumped in my hold, I used both hands to lay her on the ground. Fuck the bed, I needed her now and I kicked off my pants. Good thing I hadn't bothered with briefs. My patience was gone. Her arms were spread over her head as she tried to come to her senses.

"Now I'm going to fuck you until you pass out." That was a fucking promise.

My dick was so hard, it was nearly purple with need. The head was thick and like a rod as I lined up to drive in. She was so wet, I didn't have to shove my way in, though it was a tight fit. She was swollen from her first orgasm and I had to spread her legs wider so I didn't hurt her too much. We had a long night ahead of us and I couldn't have her in pain the entire time.

She whimpered. "I don't think it... I can't..."

"You can and it will." I wanted a home run, but I was

rounding the bases as I worked it in as far as it would go. I held there, taking a cleansing breath. Her hands had formed a vice grip around my arms.

"Now," she said.

I didn't need another word. Our flesh slapped together as I drove in and out of her like a man possessed. Her pussy was heaven, and I was the devil ready to corrupt her. I arched my hips, hitting that spot that made her back rise off the floor.

Her walls were closing in on me, letting me know she was close as hell, and I hadn't even played with her clit yet.

"Don't you come," I commanded like I could order her orgasm back.

Her expression pinched as she tried to comply, but I was good at what I did. If I wanted her to wait, I would have to stop. So like the madman I was in that moment, I pulled out.

"What?" she cried, so close frustration pinched her brows.

"On your knees and suck me off."

There was an automatic challenge in her eyes. She didn't like me telling her what to do in that moment. I lifted a brow and worked a hand up and down my shaft, letting her know what I would do if she didn't.

"You're evil," she spat.

"The very worst." I loosened my tie and took my time with the buttons of my shirt as she continued to stare me down. "If you want my cock, you'll suck until I say stop."

Her jaw dropped as I pulled off my tie and then my shirt.

"Yes, just like that. A little wider though. I'm a big boy."

She didn't move, which turned me on. I was used to getting what I wanted, when I wanted it, at work and in the bedroom, though we were on her living room floor at the moment.

I got her attention as I fisted my cock on a groan. "Yes, I can get myself off and leave you like that," I said.

She sat up and slid a hand from between her beautiful tits down to her pussy. "I can take care of myself too."

Her pout was cute, but she wasn't fooling either one of us.

"Nothing beats my dick. You know that and so do I."

She ground her teeth and then fell forward on her hands to crawl toward me with an evil glance.

"Bite me and I'll come down your throat and won't touch you for the rest of the night."

She didn't answer, only reached up for my cock. I let myself go as she fisted me as best she could. The grip she had only added to my excitement. When she complied and took the head into her mouth, I said, "Good girl. Taste yourself. Isn't it sweet?"

In agreement, she sucked me in further, swirling her tongue on the underside of my shaft. She was a crafty little minx and I wanted her like there was no tomorrow.

I was getting closer and wanted in her again. "Turn around and show me your pretty ass."

She wanted me to fuck her. I saw it in her eyes as she backed away before doing as I asked.

I got to my knees, sliding a hand over her back before giving her a light tap on the ass. She wiggled it and moaned.

I took her hips and drove so hard and fast into her, I stole her breath. Then I moved again. My dick was so sensitive, I fought to hang on until she was spasming around me. I gave in and came inside her.

She practically collapsed to the floor. I scooped her up

and took her to the bedroom, where we both fell onto the bed and I pulled her close.

"I suppose that means we are going to try the natural way?"

"Damn right. I'm going to fuck you, but to make sure, we'll go to a specialist to test your readiness and do whatever's necessary to ensure you're pregnant."

She nodded and we both drifted off to sleep.

I woke to the shrill sound of her voice. She hovered over me with something small in her hand. "You're Hugh Hampton with Hampton's Media. My friend Chloe's asshole boss!"

It took a moment to realize she had my business card I'd left for her the other day. I nodded, also making the connection with Chloe, my most valuable employee.

"Wait, I can explain," I said when I saw the hatred in her eyes. That told me Chloe wasn't my biggest fan.

"No." She shook her head. "You have to leave now. The deal's off, you bastard. How dare you come here?" She said that like I'd planned this against her friend.

"I had no fucking clue you knew Chloe. She's my best employee."

Her finger was aimed at me like she wanted to claw my eyes out. I scooted off the bed, well aware my dick was swinging in the breeze.

"Don't you dare, you asshole. You were fucking your admin. Chloe caught you. And you're here fucking me." She shuddered. "You better not have some disease or I'm suing the hell out of you."

"I didn't fuck her without protection, only you."

Her hair fanned around her head from the way she was shaking it. "Get the fuck out or I'm calling the cops."

I eased around her and pulled on my pants and my

shirt, not bothering with buttoning it as she glared at me. "I can make this right," I pleaded.

She wasn't having any of it. I grabbed my tie and headed for the door. I held there a second, hoping she'd change her mind. But she didn't. It slammed as I headed for my car. Good thing I'd driven. I got another evil glare from a mother who covered her daughter's eyes as I jogged to the car, shirt flapping in the breeze.

FIVE

Molly

When the door slammed behind him, I was sure the door to my future slammed as well. My hand shook as I parted the blinds and watched him get into his expensive car. He didn't drive away immediately, as I'd thought he would. He sat behind the wheel for a few minutes, and then his fists crashed into that same wheel. I feared for a minute his anger would have him ripping the thing apart. But a few moments later, he drove off, tires spinning as he went.

Had I made the biggest mistake of my life? Probably, but I didn't know what else to do. Staying with him was a betrayal of the worst sort to Chloe, and I couldn't have that. Why hadn't I looked at the card he'd left on the counter? I'd let myself get all worked up over the possibilities of a better life for Mom and the chance of Dad getting out of prison. Now it vanished like a wisp of smoke.

My butt hit the chair at my pitiful kitchen table, and I slumped in the seat. It would have to be the one directly in front of the pile of bills that were stealing my life away. The questions about both my parents pounded my brain. Mom was too young to be in a nursing home. And Dad was far too honest to have embezzled any money.

Self-pity took over, which was unusual for me. I wasn't one to give in to those feelings because I viewed them as a waste of time and energy, but today had been a huge disappointment. To top it off, the person who could usually pull me out of my sour mood was off-limits. There wasn't a chance in hell I could talk to Chloe about this.

My phone rang, jolting me out of this sad state of affairs. Maybe it was the lottery calling to tell me I'd won a million dollars. Fat chance, even though I'd been entering that stupid thing for God only knew how long now.

Only it wasn't. It was my mom, which only made my heart crack even more. Bolstering my spirits for what would be a long, sad conversation, I answered it with as much cheer as I could muster. "Hi, Mom."

"Hi, darling." The words were slurred and barely recognizable. I was used to her speech by now, so I understood her.

"How are you today?"

"I'm fine. How is my favorite daughter?"

"I'm your only daughter." I laughed, not because I felt it, but because I hoped it would cheer her.

"But you are my favorite too. Are you having fun?"

"Yes, Mom. Lots of fun. I'm coming to visit you the day after tomorrow. On Saturday."

"Oh, Molly, don't waste time driving out here. I want you to live your life and not spend it on me."

"Mom, visiting you is not a waste of my time."

"I'd rather you be meeting a nice young man so I could

have a grandchild before I leave this earth. And you won't meet one visiting your mother in a nursing home."

Her words gave me pause and made me think about Hugh and his offer again. Had I royally screwed up by kicking him out? With his money, I could move Mom closer, which would lessen the burden of me having to drive so far to see her. I could then visit her more often. It would also make Mom happy to have the grandchild she'd always dreamed of having. Dad could have a better legal team at his disposal. If his name were cleared, he could possibly go back to work.

There would still be the issue of telling Chloe, but maybe I could get by without naming the father of the baby. I might be able to tell her I didn't know who it was—that it had happened while I was sleeping with two men and I didn't want to divulge their names. Nah, she'd never buy it. Lying to her also wasn't an option. I would be honest and tell her I hadn't known who he was at first. I could only hope she would forgive me this business deal, because that was all it really was.

"Molly, honey, are you still there?"

"Yeah, Mom, I'm here. I'd love to give you a grandchild and maybe I will someday. But I still want to visit you. You're my mother and I love you dearly. So stop telling me not to come."

"You always were persistent."

I was, wasn't I. I changed the subject. "Hey, Mom, they treat you good over there, don't they?"

"Yes, dear."

"And you'd tell me if they didn't?"

"I would."

"Okay. Then I'll see you Saturday around lunch. I love you, Mom."

"Love you too, dear."

As soon as the call ended, I hunted for Hugh's card. His name burned a hole in my hand as I stared at it. This would be the most difficult decision of my life. There was a lot riding on this, but if I did the right thing, my parents could really benefit from this. And so could I.

In the morning, when I arrived at work, there was a huge bouquet of flowers sitting on my desk along with a box of expensive chocolates and another box. There wasn't a card or anything else accompanying them. I asked around and no one had seen the delivery person. Who could've sent these? Was it Hugh? But why after the way I'd treated him?

The answer to that question lay in the box. There was only one person who would have sent me that.

The rest of the day went to shit because he was all I thought of. Why hadn't I taken the time to listen to his explanation? I'd just kicked him out, assuming the worst. That was so unlike me. I wasn't sure who I was more pissed off at—him or me.

Hugh

Earlier…

What the hell had happened back there? I'd left that card in her apartment the other day. How had she not seen it? How was I supposed to know Chloe was her best friend and Chloe thought I was an asshole? What had I done to deserve that? I'd thought I treated her well. I gave her all sorts of responsibilities at work. She was my best employee and I trusted her with everything, which was why I gave her the most difficult tasks to do. Where had this all gone so damn wrong? Here I'd thought I had it all figured out. Now what the fuck was I supposed to do?

I rammed my hands against the steering wheel in frustration. At this point I was at a loss. A change of plans was in order, but where would I begin? I had everything lined up for Molly. I couldn't start all over. She was the one—the chosen mother of my future heir. I had to come up with a solution... and fast.

Wait! I was a master planner, a creative genius. Wasn't I the one who'd come up with the idea for Hampton's Media? Hadn't I taken it from the ground up to what it was today? I had the ability to turn things around with Molly too. I wasn't going to lie down and give up. No way. She would hear me out if it was the last thing I ever did.

But what would I tell her? The truth, which was what exactly? I had to find a way to get her to listen. I made a phone call and enlisted the aid of someone I could get answers from. I knew it was only a start, but when Molly went to work in the morning, she would find a big surprise waiting for her.

Next, I had to examine what was going on in my own office. That little affair I'd had with the admin had certainly been a huge error, and I didn't intend to make that same mistake again. If Molly gave me a chance, I wouldn't have to worry about it. As far as Chloe went, I needed to understand why she thought I was such an ass.

After digging around a bit and speaking to a few of the other employees, it seemed by giving her some of the most important assignments, I had overloaded her with work. It hadn't been intentional. I just hadn't kept track of what I'd assigned to her, which was careless on my part. I owed her a huge apology, and a raise. She'd been working like a dog and I hadn't shown her the appreciation she deserved.

However, on Monday, Chloe came in and resigned. She gave me a piece of her mind, telling me what a shit boss I was. I never had time to make amends before she cleaned out her desk and was gone. I was fucked. Despite feeling awful for how I'd treated her because my head had been wrapped up in the games my family played, I knew this could work against me with Molly. If I didn't make things right with Chloe, I could lose the opportunity for a future with Molly. Besides, Chloe was by far the best employee I had.

My phone rang a few minutes later.

"Mr. Hampton, the flowers were delivered, along with the first of your gifts, to Miss Coleman."

"Ah, perfect. Thank you, Wilson. The tip I gave you paid off?"

I'd called Dillon, the guy who'd hosted the party where Molly and I had met. He remembered Molly by the description I'd given of her. Apparently, I hadn't been the only guy interested. Damn good thing I'd made my move when I had. Dillon had given me a name I'd passed on.

"Yes, I contacted Joe, the individual she was with on Friday at the party. He said he would be happy to help, but he wouldn't divulge any personal information about her."

"Will he be discreet?"

"I believe so. He seems a bit desperate for money."

"Are they only good friends?"

"He assures me they are only friends."

"As long as he can be trusted then go ahead with the plan."

"Yes, sir. I shall call you when Joe has something arranged."

"Thank you, Wilson."

This Joe, whoever he was, better be on the up and up,

and better not fuck anything up for me. I only had Wilson's word to go on, but he was very astute when it came to judging people. Wilson had been working for me for several years and was quite loyal.

Molly

The next day as I drove home from the nursing home, I realized exactly how much better it would be if Mom were closer. Hugh's offer screamed in my head. But what if I was too late? What if he were so angry with me, he decided that I was a terrible choice? I wouldn't know the answer to that unless I asked.

His card was on my table where I'd left it, next to the flowers and empty box of chocolates. I'd eaten those while trying to decide what to do. Now I picked up his card and it almost glared back at me. Was that a challenge? Because I never backed down from a challenge. Before I lost the courage, I tapped in his number.

"Hampton."

"Uh, Hugh, this is Molly."

"Molly?"

"Er, yes, Molly."

"What can I do for you?"

I guessed I'd really messed up. He sounded so cold with the formality of his question. Like what else could I be calling about? I pushed ahead anyway. "Yeah, well, I've been thinking. I may have acted a bit too hastily the other day."

"And?" he prompted, not giving an inch.

"Um, well, first I should say, you shouldn't have, and I can't accept." I was referring to the unexpected gift in the box.

"Why not? I need you to stay healthy while you're deciding on what to do."

"You still want me to give you an heir after everything?"

He was silent a second. "Yes," he said, and continued with, "You can use that gift card to buy food and vitamins. I would have paid your bills, but I thought you'd think it an invasion of your privacy."

"Yes, it would have been. I'm grateful you didn't. But still, we should talk first. Would you be willing to come over so we can discuss it?"

"Actually, I think it would be better if we met for dinner."

"Dinner?"

"Yes, dinner. That's when you go to an eating establishment and order food. Are you familiar with that?" He was teasing me, which gave me hope.

"No, I don't think I am," I said, deciding to play along.

"Good. That'll give me an opportunity to teach you something then. My driver will pick you up at seven. I'll see you tonight."

I had a decision to make when the call ended. It was made that evening when I stressed over what to wear. I'd never bothered to ask Hugh where we were going, so I didn't know if I should dress up or not. I ended up wearing a simple, yet semi-dressy black dress with a neckline that dipped a bit low, revealing a hint of my cleavage. Maybe that would entice him a little. I also made sure to wear a sexy black lacy bra with a matching thong, just in case.

What the hell was I thinking? This was supposed to be a business arrangement. I wasn't out to seduce the man. Or was I? Was I trying to worm my way into his good graces again through sex? Was I that desperate for money? The answer was yes.

When my doorbell rang, I was disappointed to see it wasn't him standing there, but rather a stranger wearing a chauffeur's uniform.

"Miss Coleman, I'm Ned, Mr. Hampton's driver. Are you ready?"

"Yes."

"Excellent. Follow me, please."

He ushered me to a black limo in the parking lot and I slid into the luxurious back seat. Immediately, all thoughts of how much money this man had assaulted my brain. I would have to be on my best behavior to win him over tonight.

The limousine stopped in front of one of the ritziest restaurants in town. I'd never eaten there before because it was way out of my league in price. I was immediately happy I'd chosen the black dress to wear. Ned opened the door and informed me Mr. Hampton already waited inside. My stomach fluttered, but I squelched my nerves and stiffened my spine. Nothing would deter me from my mission tonight. By the time I made it inside, the imminent anxiety eased, and I was much more in control.

"May I help you, miss?" the hostess asked.

"Yes. I'm meeting a Mr. Hampton here for dinner."

"Ah, yes. Follow me please."

The restaurant was an old establishment, and it was sectioned off in a multitude of private cubicles. We weaved our way around until we arrived at Hugh's table. He stood and seated me. "You look lovely tonight, Molly."

"Thank you. So do you." And he did. He was wearing a navy suit, a crisp white shirt, and a patterned blue tie. "I have to admit, I didn't know what to wear since I had no idea where we were eating tonight."

"I'm sorry. I should've told you."

"No, it's fine. I've always wanted to eat here."

"This is your first time?" he asked.

"Yes."

"Then I'm happy I chose it. Tell me, why the change of heart? I was sure from the way you sent me away you'd never want to speak to me again."

I cringed at his words. He was right. I had treated him poorly. I guessed there was no use beating around the bush, so I might as well jump right into my explanation. But as I was getting ready to open my mouth, a gorgeous woman walked up to our table and said, "Well, if it isn't Hugh Hampton."

SIX

Hugh

"Claudia," I said.

I didn't introduce my silent partner as she eyed Molly like she was a stain on the chair before turning her attention to me.

"I see things haven't changed," she said to me while pretending Molly didn't exist. The things I wanted to say were held back because the damn woman had me by the balls. I clenched my teeth and bit back cursing her to hell, where she'd come from. Claudia had been a mistake my dick hadn't seen coming, in more ways than one. In my bid to start my business, she'd offered some capital. Things had been good between us then and that had turned out to be one of the biggest mistakes of my life. Now I shared my corporation with her.

She kept glancing at Molly as if I should introduce her. But it was better for me and especially Molly if Claudia didn't know anything about her.

"I'm in the middle of a meeting. If you'd like to chat, I can have my assistant work with yours on a suitable time."

"Touché," Claudia muttered. "We do need to get together. I got a call I think you'll be interested in hearing about." Then, on pencil-thin heels, she clicked away.

"And that was?" Molly waited for an answer.

"An error in judgment." The words slipped from my mouth and her brows drew up. I amended my statement. "No one you need to worry about. And trust me, it's best you don't know her. She's a viper in human skin."

Molly waved it away. "I'm not sure why I asked. What you do is your business."

Grateful she'd given me an out, I pulled out a bound document and set it in front of her.

"What's this?" she asked.

"Our agreement."

Something like betrayal crossed her features when our eyes met. "We need this?"

"It's for your protection. If you have my child and something happens to me, everything I've promised to you is written down and will supersede a will." I tapped it with an index finger. "In summary, I'll give you this in good faith." I pulled out a check and slid it across to her. Her eyes nearly bugged out when she saw the sum. "Then when you go to have tests run to check your health and the ability to conceive, I'll give you this." I opened up the portfolio and pointed to the summary schedule of payments. "As you see, by just doing the tests, you will have earned enough money to pay the bills I saw."

She licked her lips and quietly said, "I can't believe I'm saying this, but that won't cover everything."

I nodded. "Once you are confirmed pregnant by a doctor of my choosing, you will receive this amount, which should be enough to take you out of financial debt and secure your financial wellbeing for the long term."

She glanced up with almost childlike concern. "And what if I miscarry?"

"Everything I've given to you up to that point is yours to keep, including the gift card. If you give birth, there is a final lump sum. Then a monthly stipend will be given to you and each child."

"Each child?"

But then we were interrupted by the waiter. It was another ten minutes before we came back to our conversation.

"Each child?" she repeated when we were alone again.

"We'll be going to a fertility doctor," I said. "It's possible they will give you hormones that could increase the chance of multiple births." She sat back. "Don't worry, you and any child we have together will be well taken care of, including a nanny or nannies if needed."

She nodded. "So if we are going to a fertility doctor, does that mean they'll artificially put your sperm into me?"

"Hell, no," I said a little too loudly. A few patrons turned our way. I lowered my voice. "I won't take a chance there's a screwup and they put the wrong sperm in you."

"Better for you."

"Better for us. I think I've proven that."

Her lips twitched.

"There is one thing I should point out. From this moment forward, your pretty pussy is mine. I can't chance that someone else will get you pregnant." When she started to balk, I pointed at the check in front of her. "I think you've been properly compensated for your time."

"That makes me sound like a hooker."

"No, that makes you more like a surrogate." That was

the wrong thing to say as I watched her cringe. "I didn't mean it that way, though if you are found to be an unfit mother, I will retain full custody." Her back stiffened. "I don't see that as a problem. And if you do, you will see that it's language to protect our child. The language goes both ways. If you feel I'm unfit, you can seek full custody."

She relaxed some and flipped through the pages like she was shuffling cards. "Why so many pages?"

I shrugged. "My lawyer drafted it. You can have a lawyer of your choosing review it. And with this first payment, you should have enough money to pay for one. But I will cover that expense as you need that money for more urgent matters. Just send me the bill."

She nodded. "So what's next?"

"Besides dinner?"

She laughed some. "Yes, besides dinner."

I pulled up my phone. "I have an app that can assist figuring out when you'll be ovulating after you answer a few questions."

"Seriously?"

"No need to be shy now. We will be parents. I need to know when your last period was."

She turned a lovely shade of red that made my dick uncomfortably hard. But she answered that and several more questions.

"It looks like this coming weekend you'll ovulate. We need to get those tests run tonight."

She pointed at her chest. "Just me?"

I shook my head. "Me too. You need assurances just like I do."

"That's magnanimous of you."

"That's selfish of me. I want inside of you with nothing between us as soon as possible. In fact, after tonight, you will be in my bed every night until I'm positive you're pregnant with my child."

Her brow arched. I lifted my glass of Scotch and sipped.

Then I added, "Unless you want to rip up that check and walk away."

SEVEN

Molly

Tests. Ovulating. Sleeping with him every night. As the saying went, this shit was getting real. Then I reminded myself about Mom, the stack of bills, and Dad sitting behind bars.

"I'm not going anywhere. I'm in." I pulled my gaze away from my knotted fingers up to his magnificent silver-gray eyes. I found myself drowning in them as my worries about Mom and Dad faded away. All I could remember was Hugh sliding in and out of me, and how amazing the sex had been. I crossed my legs, hoping that would ease the building pressure. "Um..." I cleared my throat. "I also don't have a problem sleeping with you either."

A smile grew across his face. "Good. Then shall we proceed?"

"Proceed?"

"With our plans?"

"Oh, right." My heart thudded in my chest.

"Don't be nervous, Molly. I can't be that bad."

"No, it's not that."

"Then what?"

"What will I tell Chloe? She's bound to call and wonder what's happened to me."

He leaned across the table and picked up one of my hands. "Don't worry about Chloe. She no longer works for me. And when the time comes, we'll figure something out."

"I wonder why she hasn't called me," I mused out loud. I couldn't believe she'd quit and hadn't said anything to me.

"Why don't we run by your place after dinner so you can pack a few things, since you'll be spending your nights with me?"

My thoughts raced as words froze on my tongue. How awkward was this going to be? I would basically be living with him until my pregnancy was confirmed.

"What's running around in that head of yours?"

"Nothing, other than figuring out what I need to bring."

"You sure about that?"

Why was he so observant? "Yes, I'm sure."

Our food arrived and the waiter asked if we needed anything else. Since my brain was so addled, Hugh had ordered for me. That was something I never let a man do, but he did not disappoint. Sitting before me was a lovely filet mignon and a mouthwatering stuffed baked potato. When I cut into the steak, it was cooked to perfection.

"How is everything?"

"Delicious." I practically moaned the words. I never ate like this, being on the tight budget that I was.

"I'm glad you're enjoying it."

I polished off my plate without even noticing that he was watching me eat. At least not until I finished and looked up to see him staring at me. I wiped my mouth with the crisp linen napkin and immediately stared down at my empty plate.

"I'm sorry," I said in a hushed tone.

"Whatever for?"

"I inhaled my food and didn't talk much."

"You enjoyed a good meal and that's important, especially if you'll be carrying my child. Besides, I hate to see a woman pick at her food. It's extremely annoying. You buy a dinner, you ought to eat the damn thing."

I jerked up to see his mouth twitching with humor, and I laughed with him. He didn't seem to be an overly lighthearted guy, so I was seeing a different side to him, and I liked it.

"You won't have to worry about that with me. I enjoy eating, as you can probably tell."

"What's that supposed to mean?"

I aimed my thumb toward my hips. "I'm not one of those super skinny girls. That's all."

"You look perfect to me and that's all that counts."

I took the compliment. I was never happy with my body, but then again, what woman was?

We finished our wine and Hugh paid the bill. For once, I didn't worry about the price of the meal. What a great feeling it was, too.

Hugh escorted me outside and we waited for the valet to return with his car.

"No driver tonight?" I asked as we waited.

"No, I drove."

A few minutes later, a silver Bentley pulled up. Hugh helped me inside and the scent of leather filled my nostrils. I'd never been in a car this fancy, other than the limo that had brought me here. Too bad this was only going to be temporary.

"Nice wheels," I said.

"Thanks." He pressed a button and we sped off toward my apartment. It didn't take long to get there, as the restaurant was fairly close. I would've liked to stay in the car because the seats were more comfortable than my bed.

"You coming up, or do you want to just wait out here?" I asked.

"I'll join you, if you don't mind."

"I don't mind. I promise to be quick."

We went inside and I threw some items into a small suitcase, like makeup, shampoo, a blow dryer, and then clothing I'd need for the next day for work. It didn't take long at all.

On the way back to Hugh's, I said, "Good thing I don't have a cat."

"Why's that?"

"I'd have to bring him along."

"You could've done that. I like pussy," he said with a poker face.

"Oh, my God. I can't believe you said that."

"It's true." Then I noticed the grin tugging at the corners of his mouth.

"You don't laugh much, do you?" I asked.

He gave me a sidelong glance for a second, then turned his gaze back to the road. "Why do you ask?"

"Because you seem so serious."

"I laugh."

"Not much. Admit it."

"All right. You're correct. I don't," he said.

"Why not?" It made me curious about him.

He drummed his fingers on the wheel. "I'm usually preoccupied with work."

"Stressful, huh?" I asked.

"I wouldn't know where to begin, but you don't need to hear it."

"If you ever want to talk, I'm available. I'm pretty sure my picture appears under the word 'stress' in the dictionary, so I can probably relate. Maybe not in the same sense, but stress is stress, yeah?"

He checked me out again and nodded. "Thanks. I appreciate that."

I became aware of the part of town we had entered when Hugh turned into a parking garage. "Is this where you live?"

"In the building adjacent to this. Pay close attention because if you ever drive here, you'll have a designated parking spot."

I watched to see where we went and noticed that every spot was numbered. When we got out of the car, Hugh pointed to the space that would be mine. "Right there. That will be assigned to you for as long as we're together."

"Okay." I couldn't imagine driving my clunker up here. It wasn't exactly a clunker, but compared to all the other cars it was. There was more money parked here than I'd ever have in my bank account for the rest of my life.

Hugh placed his hand on my back and led me to a walkway that connected to the next building. Then we stepped into an elevator. He used a key card, passed it over an electronic pad, and pushed the *PH* button. *Shit.* He lived in the freakin' penthouse.

The elevator opened up into a foyer, which led to another set of doors. On the wall was a keypad, and he entered a series of numbers. When we heard the beep, we walked through into the most magnificent room I'd ever seen. It rivaled the house where I'd met him.

"Whoa. This is unreal." I headed straight to the glass

wall that overlooked the city. The room was huge and very modern, but it was the view that captured my attention.

"This is exactly why I bought the place. Once I saw the view, I couldn't stop thinking about it." Then he turned to me and said, "You enhance it that much more."

Gone was the businessman and in his place was the guy who'd swept me away. Contracts were forgotten as his mouth took possession of mine. The only thing spinning around in my head was that I wanted—needed—this man.

Both of his hands gripped my ass and lifted me up. My legs wrapped around his waist as he walked me to his bedroom. I was so into the kiss, I didn't notice my surroundings. Damn, the man could kiss. His tongue tangled with mine, twisting up my emotions in the process. My stomach was alive with a million fluttering butterflies, and my skin was on fire for his touch.

He set me on the bed, and I kicked off my shoes. My dress was up to my thighs as he spread my legs wide. Heat rolled off me as the passion flared between us. His smooth skin was begging to be touched, so I sank my nails into the collar of his shirt and pulled with all my might. The buttons went flying, pinging off the wooden floor.

"I really liked that shirt."

"I didn't," I said. "It was in the way." His throaty chuckle sent shivers racing across my skin. "See, I knew you could laugh."

He tugged my dress and bra down, exposing a diamond-hard nipple. "Only you seem to be able to make me laugh."

"Your laugh does this to me." I pointed to my erect nipple.

"Then I'll have to laugh more. I didn't know it had that kind of effect on you." His lips clamped down, sucking hard, and I moaned. I pinched the other one, because I was so ready for him to make me his. This dress was too cumbersome and only getting in the way, so I shimmied my hips, trying to get the thing off.

"Are you that impatient?" he asked.

"I want to be naked with you."

"Let me do the honors." He grabbed the hem of my dress and pulled it off. My bra followed next, freeing my aching nipples. I was left lying in my thong as he stared at me. I reached for his belt, but he stepped away, taking his time by teasing me while he stripped.

"You're not fair."

"Who said anything about being fair?"

I licked my lips when his rock-hard cock sprang free of its prison and my mouth immediately watered. Sitting up, I motioned for him to come closer. "Let me suck you off."

"As much as I would love that, there's not a chance in hell I'm wasting a drop of my sperm down that pretty throat of yours."

His comment reminded me all too well that this was merely a business transaction to him, another contractual obligation. I nodded and lay back down.

He tugged my thong off, and his mouth dove down onto my pussy. He was out to conquer and that he did. His tongue worked me over like I'd never been. Every part of me was expertly massaged until I fired off two orgasms. Only my mind had wandered off into the land of obligations. I had hoped we'd crossed a bridge, spanned a gap where maybe we could work something out. If we did have a child together, I wanted us to be more than casual acquaintances.

"On your knees, Molly. I want to give it to you hard."

But he was wrong. He'd already given it to me. In the form of a check. Or so I thought.

His thick, hard cock slowly, achingly entered me and

stole my breath away. I'd thought I was prepared, but I was wrong. Hugh Hampton turned me into a fuck monster. When he started moving to that rhythm, I lost all sense and the only thing I could think of was the pleasure he was giving me. It was sublime.

"Yes, yes, just like that." He was touching me in places no man had ever done.

He mounded up some pillows then pushed me down on them. "Here, how's this?"

"Perfect. Fuck me hard."

"How hard?"

"As hard as you can."

And he did. He drilled into me over and over as I yelled out my orgasm. "Ahhh, that's so goooood."

He kept going. "I love going bare with you, baby. You're the only woman I've done this with."

"Oh, yesss."

"Molly, use your hand. I'm close and I want to feel you squeeze my cock as I come. I want you to take all of me."

I did as he asked and brought myself to another climax. He came when I did, shouting my name.

About that time, my phone rang. My purse, which had been on my shoulder, was on the bed with us and my phone had fallen out of the front pocket. I grabbed it to shut it off, but then I saw who was calling. "Shit, it's Chloe."

"Don't worry, just let it go to voicemail."

"Yeah, I will."

But then a text came through right after and it too was from Chloe.

Damn, girl, who are you doing tonight? He sure must be something from the sounds of it. Haha. Thanks for the butt dial.

EIGHT

Hugh

Plans were taking shape. Mine in the form of Joe. He would be bringing Molly to me for a private lunch.

I'd tried to talk to Chloe. So far, she wouldn't return my calls. My next option would be to see her in person. I had to get through morning meetings first so I could see Molly.

She was quickly becoming my obsession. Fucking her was better than anything known to man. I was addicted.

"Mr. Hampton."

I glanced up and found my assistant. "Yes," I said.

"You have a visitor."

There wasn't a meeting on my calendar. "Who is it?"

"He won't say other than you'll want to meet him."

Ryan. "Send him in."

She left and seconds later, sure enough, my cousin and competitor in the heir game strolled through the door like he owned the place. "You're going soft, cousin," he announced.

"Why are you here?"

"Why else? I'm on my way to producing the first heir and thought I should warn you."

"How magnanimous of you."

He waved me off. "Don't act like I put us in this position. You were like a brother to me."

"And yet here you are, throwing victory in my face."

"No, I'm here to warn you about the woman you're thinking of having a child with."

My vision tunneled down to slits. "How would you know anything?"

"I have my sources."

I could only think of one person who'd seen me with Molly and would know that information would be interesting to Ryan. "Claudia," I said out loud.

"Not exactly. But let me tell you this. This woman you are fucking wouldn't pass Grandfather's background checks. I tell you this because no matter what, I don't want to see you get burned."

Grandfather wasn't alive, but when he had been, he'd had a nasty way of checking into people who came close to our family, including friends and lovers.

"You came all this way to give me that cryptic message?"

Ryan stood. "Let's just say her family has intimate knowledge of the prison system." Then he left, leaving me wondering how I could have let my dick rule over my brain. I'd trusted a woman I didn't know.

When it was time to meet said woman for lunch, I decided it would be a different kind of meeting than I'd initially planned. The private room I'd booked wouldn't be for a lunchtime fucking session with food as a side item. Things would be very different from my original plans.

I sat, hands steepled, tapping them as I went over what

I'd learned. A simple Google search had revealed much. I didn't need an investigator to find out more.

Molly walked in with Joe bidding her goodbye behind her. "Wow, you did this?" She stared at the table, elegantly set with the finest crystal, Waterford china, and silverware for two with a single rose bud set in the middle.

The asshole in me wanted to remain sitting. But I stood and helped her in her chair.

"You seem tense?" she said, sounding nervous.

I took my time before answering as I sat back down. "Is there anything you want to tell me?"

Her brows furrowed in confusion. "I don't think so."

"About your family?" I said. Her eyes widened. "Some information came my way and I Googled you."

She glanced away. "I meant to tell you—"

"But you didn't."

Her head snapped back so she could glare at me. "My father is innocent, and I'll do whatever is necessary to help prove that."

"Including having a kid with me?"

Her lips pursed as she lifted her chin.

"I could've gotten past that. But that wasn't the only thing that came up with the search. There are links to a bad accident. Your mother has been left unable to take care of herself from it. As tragic as that is, it's the part about her history with seizures that you should have shared with me."

"I—I," she said, tripping over the one word. "I didn't think about it being hereditary. I've never had a seizure in my life."

"Still, I'm left to wonder how I can trust you, since you didn't share those details that might affect our child's future. If your father loses his case, then what? If our child has seizures and dies..." I held up my hands in question.

She covered her mouth. "I never thought—" She got to her feet. "Look, we'll just call it off."

I should let her walk away, but I couldn't. I was two steps behind her until I managed to catch her at the door. I spun her around and pinned her there. "It's too fucking late. You could be pregnant already. I have enough money to get our child the best treatment possible. But if you lie to me again, this is over."

I crushed my lips to hers, ready to invade her mouth. She tasted like wintermint gum, which burst on my tongue. I would have fucked her there except someone knocked.

"Sir."

I pulled back. We were both gasping. Sparks flew from her eyes, and I wasn't sure if I'd lost her with my little rant.

We stepped back so the waiter could enter. "Your first course is ready to be served," he said.

"I didn't order anything," Molly said.

"I took the liberty of ordering for both of us, seeing as you have to get back to work. But feel free to tell the chef if you would prefer something else."

Her gaze shifted over to the open door where a team of people stood in the hallway. "Sorry," she muttered to them and went back to her seat.

Our gazes were fused as the meal was placed in front of us. The chef explained the dish. It wasn't until everyone left that Molly spoke.

NINE

Molly

The array of beautiful dishes that sat in front of me should've been tempting, but my appetite had gone up in smoke with Hugh's words. He was right. I should have told him. I'd wanted to but had pushed it to the back of my mind. However, the way he'd confronted me pissed me off something fierce.

"Why aren't you eating?" His voice pulled me back to the problem at hand.

"I'm not hungry. We need to clear the air if what we're doing is going to work."

"Going to work? Molly, you and I have fucked numerous times. There is no doubt it's going to work. It's only a matter of time before one of my sperm finds one of your eggs."

I frowned and the glare I sent him should've made him quiver. It didn't. He smirked, then chuckled instead. "I enjoy seeing this spirited side of you."

"I don't enjoy feeling this way. One, I'm sorry I didn't tell you about my father. I fully intend to see him released, one way or another. My dad is incapable of doing anything like that. He would never in a million years embezzle money from his lifelong business partner. Two, my mom is far too young to be confined to the state she is in and for you to bring that up is horrible." Tears threatened to bubble out, but I refused to give in to them. "The last year and a half has been hell and I've spent every cent I've earned on my parents. You want to know why I'm in such debt? You have your answer. Don't be so quick to judge when you haven't lacked for money a day in your life."

He dabbed his mouth with the napkin and set it down. "I wasn't judging—"

"Really? It sure felt that way to me. And what if we have a child who has seizures? Will you not love him or her because he's flawed?"

Hugh's mouth opened, then closed. He finally said, "I would love any child of mine, Molly, no matter what." Then he stood, walked around the table and pulled me into his arms. "If I really felt the way you say, I'd walk out of this room and never glance back." His mouth feverishly met mine, leaving me helpless in his arms. Every comment, remark, argument I planned to make disappeared as lust took over. The only thing I wanted now was his cock inside of me.

He pushed my skirt up and ripped off my panties while I reached for his zipper. My hands shook, so he brushed them aside and did the work himself. Usually, he would see if I was ready, but not this time. I was lifted up and when I wrapped my legs around him, his thick cock pushed inside of me.

Somehow we ended up against a wall where he banged

me like a piston. I wanted to scream, shout, yell, but knew that was out of the question. Instead, I bit down on his shoulder to muffle the noise. No doubt there would be teeth marks, but I didn't care. My clit was getting the attention it deserved and I finally caught the orgasm I chased. It battered against me in wave after wave, over and over, leaving me breathless and weak.

With one final plunge, Hugh's warmth spread inside me, telling me he'd gotten his due. We'd both worked up a sweat, but him more than me. I lifted my head off his shoulder to see the lipstick marks I'd left and, much to my horror, blood seeped through his shirt. "Oh, God, I'm sorry."

"For what?"

"I bit you."

His body rumbled with a deep chuckle. "You certainly did, but it was well worth it."

When I moved the shirt over to get a look, there was a perfect indentation of my teeth, top and bottom. "Make sure you clean that so it doesn't get infected."

"Worried about my health now, are you?"

"Well, yeah." I didn't want to be the cause of him getting sick.

His eyes met mine, and then his lips. It was hard to deny the deep attraction between us. When it came to fucking, we were an A-plus.

"We better get composed in case any of the staff come in," I suggested.

"Not quite yet. I want to make good use of my sperm." He winked.

"Good Lord, does it always have to be about making a baby?"

He frowned, a thoughtful expression coming over him. "If you're willing to put in extra time, I suppose not."

"Extra time? I'm already living with you."

"How about coming to work for me?"

"No. I would never do that. Leaving my job isn't wise. And what if things between us don't work? Then what?"

"Molly, you're not very positive."

"Haven't you listened to me? I don't have much reason to be, considering my past."

"Your past doesn't dictate your future. And when you have our baby, what then? Will you move away and raise him or her on your own? You'll have my support, of course, but what if I want to be a big part of their life? Have you given much thought to that? And what if you and I..."

"You and I what?"

"Turn into something more."

"Do you honestly think that could happen?" It was early in our relationship, but I knew one thing. Hugh Hampton was undeniably gorgeous, and I'd never been so satisfied by anyone in bed as I was with him. But did that really mean anything? I loved being with him. He was a bit mysterious, but that was probably due to the fact we knew very little about each other. In time, that part would disappear. Would the attraction hold? I sure hoped the sexual satisfaction part stayed because going back to a vibrator seemed hugely disappointing.

After I returned to work, the wheels took off in my brain and wouldn't stop spinning. Was I crazy to have moved in with him so soon? Maybe I needed to stay at my place a night or two each week, if only to keep my sanity. That was when I decided I would go home to my place that night.

I would have texted him when I got home, but damn if he didn't beat me to the punch. By the time I walked into my apartment, which now seemed terribly tiny, my phone vibrated.

Hugh: I'm home. Where are you?

Well, shit. In the little time we'd lived together, he'd gotten home after me. Wasn't this my luck?

Me: I decided to stay at my place tonight.

No response. That was odd. Usually, he texted me back immediately. As I was changing out of my work clothes, someone pounded on my door. It didn't take a genius to figure out who it was.

Hugh stood there when I opened the door and then barged inside. "Molly, what's going on?"

"Nothing. I just needed a little breathing room."

"And you can't breathe at my place?"

"Of course I can breathe there. It's just a saying."

"Then explain."

"Stop ordering me around."

"I'm not..." He stopped and frowned. "I'm sorry. I'm upset you left. Can you please explain?"

That was better. "Yes. Like I said, I needed a little breathing room or space. We've taken this really fast."

"You're having second thoughts?"

"No, it's just that the way you accosted me at lunch made me think of how things might be between us. I'll be honest, I didn't care for that and it really upset me."

"I understand and I could've handled it better, but I was upset as well when I found out. Can we at least call a truce?"

"We sort of did at the restaurant, but yes, let's." I held out my hand.

"Oh, no. I have better ways to seal that deal." His mouth

landed on mine and soon we were in the bedroom, naked. I had orgasm number one when he came right after me. That was when we heard the knock on the door.

"Who could that be?" he asked.

"I have no idea." I hopped up and threw a robe on. When I looked out the peephole, Chloe stared back at me.

"Open up, Molly, I know you're home. Your car's right outside. It's Chloe. Let me in."

Fuck. I couldn't avoid this, so I swung the door wide and she pushed past me. "I've been calling you and you haven't answered your phone. I was worried about you. What the hell is going on?"

My mouth flopped open and closed a few times and then I said, "I've been kind of busy."

"Busy? With what? You look like you've been sleeping." Then a crash and an *Oh, fuck* came from the bedroom. "Oh, my God, you have a man in your bedroom, don't you?"

"No, I... uh, that's to say, I, er..."

"Just tell her the truth, Molly."

Chloe frowned. Then Hugh walked out of the bedroom and sparks flew out of her eyes.

"What are you doing here? And not wearing a shirt." Her gaze flicked to me and I felt like a five-year-old. "Oh, shit, oh, hell. You're sleeping with him, aren't you? Tell me I'm seeing things."

I couldn't stop squirming under her penetrating glare. "I wanted to tell you, but I was afraid you'd react like this."

"Yeah, because you knew how much it would hurt me."

"Chloe, please let us explain," Hugh said.

She stuck her finger out at him. "You don't get to say a word about this. You hear me? This is between Molly and me."

"Chloe, I knew you'd react this way if I told you, which was why I didn't," I said.

"You know, you're right, Molly. I hope you two have fun together." Chloe hurried out of my apartment as I called out to her.

I sagged, but not with relief when I closed the door. Chloe and I were peas and carrots, but this exchange had put a deep ache in my heart.

He wrapped his arms around me. "You do realize this was bound to happen one day."

"Yes, I know, but her feelings were destroyed."

TEN

Hugh

How could I be this attached to a woman so quickly? But here it was. This woman had more than a firm hold on my balls. There was most certainly more, I just couldn't name it yet. My father had warned me that one day there would be a woman who would tame the wild beast inside me. And when that day came, I would fully understand why he'd married my mother.

Was this that day?

Lunch with Molly had clued me in to several things. There wasn't much she could do to make me run away. Which was why I made a call to my friend and lawyer the following day.

"Arthur, it's been a while," I said to my buddy I hadn't talked to much since his wedding.

Arthur Lattimore had been a college buddy of mine and had made it to partner of his law firm in record time. "Up to your old tricks, I bet," he said.

I chuckled. "I'd say that wife of yours has you on a short leash." I was only teasing. He was lucky to have met her in college. I envied him.

"Willingly," he admitted. "She's pregnant with number two."

"Another girl, I'll wager."

"I'll take whatever I can get. And trust me, it's worth it. You should give it a try."

"Fatherhood?"

"Husband, father, the whole shebang."

"I'll leave that to you for now. Though there is a woman I'm very interested in."

"Though you can't see me, I'm blinking rapidly because I'm not sure I heard you correctly."

"Ha, ha, ha. Look, I need a favor. Her father's in trouble and I want to help them out."

"Okay, fill me in."

I gave him the basics about how her father had been found guilty of embezzlement, but both claimed he was innocent.

"You know criminal law is not my area."

"I know. But I assume you may know the name of someone who is a really good criminal lawyer."

"Let me do some digging. What's his name again?"

I gave him her father's name. I didn't give him hers, though that would be easily found out if he looked.

"Give me a couple of days."

"Thanks. And give your wife a big sloppy kiss for me."

"I will, because I'm the only man who will ever kiss her in this lifetime and the next."

I laughed and hung up.

Later that day, I went to Chloe's. If I wanted a chance

in hell of making it work with Molly, I needed to straighten things out with her best friend.

I knocked on the door and waited. The last time I'd spoken to her, she'd quit and had given me hell for making her life at work miserable. This wasn't going to be easy, but I had to do something.

When the door opened, Chloe looked puzzled and I couldn't blame her. "Mr. Hampton, what are you doing here?"

"Uh, Chloe, are you okay? You look a little, uh, tense," I blurted without thinking it through.

"That's an understatement."

I wasn't exactly good at apologies and said, "Is there anything I can do to help?"

She blinked. "You're joking, right?"

"No, I see that you're upset about something and I was wondering if you needed help." I was blowing this big time.

"Why on earth would you wonder that?"

"Because you appear to need it," I said, extending an olive branch because she looked like she bore the weight of the world on her shoulders.

"Mr. Hampton, I worked for you for months while you treated me like a dog, heaping work on me like I was a farm animal. And here you stand asking if I need help. I needed help when you gave me impossible deadlines to meet and threatened to fire me if I didn't."

"I did that?" It was still hard to believe. She'd been my most reliable employee. She'd made all her deadlines. I'd never given a thought that my expectations were impossible.

"You need to leave."

The door shut in my face. I took a second to gather my thoughts. I didn't think I'd done a good job of explaining myself, so I knocked again, louder so she wouldn't just ignore me.

"For the love of wine and beer, who is it now? Are you planning on sleeping out here? Should I toss you a blanket or something?"

It was time to eat crow for Molly and Chloe too. "No, I was going over what you said to me and I guess I was pretty hard on you. I wanted to tell you I was sorry."

"Look, I think you'd better leave. This is too much," she said.

"But..."

She pointed to the street. "Just go." A car door slammed, and someone yelled. We looked over and she said, "Well, I should've guessed this would get worse."

"What's he doing here?" I asked, feeling like I might know.

"You can ask him yourself."

"Get away from her," Ryan snarled.

"Hold up there," Chloe said, but that didn't stop Ryan. I was so distracted, I missed Ryan's fist. He caught me square in the jaw. My head snapped back, and I had to shake it off.

I rubbed at the ache and decided not to stoop to his level. Instead, I yelled, "What the fuck are you doing? Have you lost your mind?"

"Leave her alone. Don't you even think about touching her, Hugh."

"I wasn't touching her. We were talking. I'm not like you, you asshole." It was likely Ryan hadn't told Chloe why he was fucking her.

"Ryan, I think you'd better leave," Chloe said.

"I'm not going anywhere until we've had a chance to talk," he said, before turning furious eyes on me. "Get the fuck out of here or I'll beat the shit out of you."

"You know something? You're crazy," I said, jabbing a finger at him.

"You haven't even begun to see crazy." Ryan puffed up his chest in front of Chloe. Even if I wanted to take him down a peg, kicking Ryan's ass wouldn't win me points with Chloe and maybe I'd lose some with Molly if her friend saw me as some sort of bully.

"We're not finished, Ryan," I said, warning that he wouldn't always have a woman to protect him. "And if you hurt Chloe, I'll make sure you pay."

Ryan laughed as I played the better man and walked away.

Fuck, I thought as I got into my car. That couldn't have gone any worse. I had no idea what Molly would say or do if she talked to Chloe.

By the time I got home, I was prepared for a shitstorm. Instead, Molly was in the kitchen.

"What's this?" I asked.

She turned around with the biggest grin. "I just thought, why not start our truce with a homecooked meal? I hope you like it. Sit." She ushered me to a chair.

The woman couldn't be any sexier to me when she put a plate worthy of restaurant dining in front of me. I wanted to tell her about Chloe as it appeared she hadn't talked to her yet but decided not to ruin dinner with bad news.

The meal was great. Roasted chicken and potatoes hit the spot. The green things on the plate weren't bad either.

When I finished, she waited expectantly. "That was wonderful," I said. "I could get used to it."

Her grin was huge. "Play your cards right..."

"Hopefully, you'll feel that way after I tell you about my day," I said. Though her smile dimmed, she waited patiently. "I went to see Chloe. It didn't go too well."

"Oh, man. What happened?"

"I tried to apologize, and I bungled it. Before I could fix things, Ryan showed up." I waited for her expression to change, but apparently, she didn't know who Ryan was.

"Ryan?"

"Yeah, I think she's dating a guy named Ryan. You don't know him?"

"It's news to me. I think you're mistaken."

Was I wrong? Maybe he hadn't been there to win the inheritance. I could be totally wrong. Before I explained who Ryan was, Molly came over with a seductive smile on her face.

"Time for dessert," she said, and we ended up in my bedroom.

The next morning, I got an early call from Ben, my finance guy.

"There is some chatter about someone trying to buy into your business," he said.

I had a bad feeling Ryan was trying to steal my company from underneath me. But that wasn't even the worst thing to happen. Arthur called me to come into his office. Already in a bad mood when I arrived, I wasn't all smiles.

"Don't look so pissed off," Arthur said. "I have some good news. But we should wait for Molly."

"Wait, Molly? You know her?"

"After I looked into her father's arrest, her name came up. Turns out she works here," Arthur said. Dread filled me. "Also, James McNeill is here to explain the details."

Arthur introduced me to the criminal attorney who was in the conference room with us. When Molly walked in and saw all of us, I knew she was going to eat my balls for lunch. She was pissed.

ELEVEN

Molly

The word 'anger' didn't touch what coursed through me. My insides were an inferno, ready to erupt in flames. How could he? How could he go behind my back and involve the company I worked for? No one here knew of my past or the sordid details behind my father's unfortunate incarceration. Yes, I believed he was innocent, but everything was stacked against him. I loved my father dearly, but he'd done some stupid things to help my mom and was now paying the price. My plans involved an attorney from my hometown to clear his name, not one from the company I worked for—*thank you, Hugh.*

"Molly, please take a seat," my boss said. Ironically, he was one of the partners in the firm who I'd never even met. "You obviously know Hugh, but I'd like to introduce you to James McNeill, one of the city's brightest and best criminal defense attorneys. He's looking into your father's case."

"Hello, Molly." Mr. McNeill stuck out his hand and I shook it.

Then my feet froze to the floor as I glanced around the room and noticed Hugh was there. Mr. McNeill looked at me expectantly, but someone had poured concrete on my shoes and no matter how hard I tried to move, it was impossible.

Hugh stood and came around to my side. "Are you okay?"

I blinked rapidly in succession, and then an urge to punch his teeth out came over me. When his hand gripped my elbow, the concrete on my shoes disappeared.

"I'm fine." I smiled through gritted teeth and finally sat.

Mr. Lattimore smiled. "Great, then shall we begin? I'll let James explain since he's the expert."

My nod was stiff.

"Molly, I researched your father's case and think we may have a chance," Mr. McNeill said.

"I know that. I've been working with an attorney already." My words didn't deter him.

"A bit of leeway exists since he was the co-owner of the company," Mr. McNeill continued.

My palm hit the table. "Exactly. That's what we've been saying all along. He did what he did to help with my mom's nursing home expenses and thought everything was fine."

"Ignorance is never an excuse when it comes to the law. That's not where our leeway lies," Mr. McNeill explained.

My brows hiked up. "Oh?"

"You see, I was able to get my hands on the business contract of your father's company."

"How'd you do that?"

He waved a hand. "How doesn't matter. What matters

is I did. The contract has a clause that allows each partner to take a loan against their portion of the company's assets, which is what your father did. The only thing he did wrong was not mentioning it to his partner."

"But he was going to, only he never got the chance," I cried.

"That part doesn't matter either. As long as that clause was in effect, he didn't break the law, and therefore did not embezzle money."

I was speechless. How had our attorney missed that? Oh, right. He was incompetent, that was how. "Now what?"

"I'm going to press for an appeal."

"The attorney we have said that was going to be difficult given the circumstances."

"Believe me, Molly, it's very possible. What we have to consider though is whether the judge will grant it."

"Why wouldn't he?"

Mr. McNeill shrugged. "It depends on a few things, but don't worry about that. I plan to use my connections to see it happens."

Damn, people with clout sure had advantages over those without it.

Mr. Lattimore spoke up. "Molly, I hope this eases your mind somewhat. James is the best at what he does and hopefully your father will be a free man soon."

"Yes, and thank you, sir."

"Don't thank me. Thank Hugh. He's the one who brought it to my attention."

I turned to Hugh and smiled, albeit a sour one. I was still pissed at him.

We rose to leave with James telling me I should hear from him within a week or two.

As we were walking out, Hugh asked, "Molly, can you stay a minute? I'd like a word, please."

"Uh, I have to get back to work."

"I'm sure Arthur won't mind if you stay for a few minutes."

I glanced at the door to see that everyone else was gone. "Fine."

"I get the sense you're angry."

"Great perception you have there," I snapped.

"I don't understand."

"Hugh, I can't have this conversation here. I'll be finished in another hour. I'll meet you at your place and then I'll explain."

He agreed and left. I'd never been in favor of arguing in public and my place of employment was not the ideal setting for me to launch into him over what he'd done. I'd wait it out.

Turned out to be much harder than I thought. I barely got any work done and finally left early, saying I had a headache. It was true. My temples throbbed with each breath I took. I drove around, trying to collect and arrange my thoughts. When I got to Hugh's, he still wasn't there. I had to wait another hour for him to arrive, which didn't help matters. My jaw ached from clenching my teeth.

He walked in and headed directly for the cabinet where the liquor was stored. "Sorry, just as I was leaving, something came up. I got news that someone is trying to buy out my company."

Instead of being empathetic and asking him about it, I went straight for the jugular. "How dare you tell my employer about my father! What gave you that right? No one at the firm knew and now everyone will."

He stared at me as though I'd punched him. "I was only trying to help."

"Trying to help? Then why didn't you come to me first?"

"I, uh, don't know. Arthur and I go way back so I figured he would be the perfect one to approach in this situation. I never gave it a thought that you worked at his firm."

"Right. So now he knows and what must he think of me?"

"Think of you? Why would he think any different?"

"Oh, come on, Hugh. You yourself did it. Anyone whose father is a convict gets a bad rap too. Like father, like daughter."

He scratched his head as though he were terribly confused. "While that may be true, I'm lost here, Molly. I thought what I did was a good deed and instead I get this. Not only that, when I got back to the office, I had a shitstorm brewing." He gulped down half the glass of brown liquor he'd poured.

"Yeah, well, I'm going to be facing my own shitstorm when everyone in the office finds out about this. The gossip chain will run wild and then I'll probably get accused of having an affair with one of the partners."

"What? That's insane!"

"In your mind, maybe, but not mine. When was the last time you worked with a bunch of gossiping admins?"

His mouth opened and closed several times before he answered. "You know what? I'll call James and tell him to forget it. That you don't give a shit about your father rotting away in prison. How does that sound?"

"You don't have to get nasty about it."

"Me? Me?" His voice rose with each word.

"Yes, you!"

Then the dreaded finger came out, aimed at me. "You need to calm down and focus on the issue at hand."

Oh, boy, he was right. "You know something? You're exactly right." I stomped out of the room and headed to the bedroom. Once there, I went to the closet and threw clothes into a suitcase, along with my cosmetics and everything else I needed. Then I zipped the thing shut and marched back out.

When he saw me, he ran to the door. "Where do you think you're going?"

"Home. To my apartment where I'm not accosted by some domineering asshole."

"Molly, you can't be serious."

"As a fucking heart attack." As I approached the door, he moved in front of it.

"I won't let you."

"So now you're keeping me a prisoner?"

"Of course not!"

"Then step aside, Hugh."

He crossed his arms and blocked the door. "No, I won't let you leave. You're being irrational."

That was the final straw. "If you don't move, I'm going to punch you."

He laughed. The fucker laughed at me! I'd show him. I balled up a fist and nailed him in the gut. When he doubled over, I made my escape.

TWELVE

Hugh

The woman had a great gut shot. I wheezed for air as I hadn't expected that. A part of me cursed her because I hadn't done anything wrong. She hadn't given me a chance to explain.

On the other hand, I could see how she'd felt ambushed. But so had I. I'd had no idea she'd worked for Arthur. Then again, his firm was the most prestigious in town.

Over the next week, I called, begged, knocked on her door, and she wouldn't see me. I even sent flowers. Nothing.

A man has his pride. My final act was to send her a letter. A goddamn handwritten letter sent via mail. Then I left her alone.

If she wasn't willing to hear me out, what more could I do?

The next sucker punch came when I was informed my ex had sold her shares in my company to Ryan. My cousin, the man I'd once thought of a brother, had won.

After two weeks waiting patiently for Molly to cool off, I lost it from this news. I hit bottom and spent the next three nights on a bender, calling out sick to my admin. I'd lost it all. My company and Molly.

The woman had burrowed deep in my heart in a matter of weeks. I saw her everywhere in my house even though she'd only lived here a short time. I missed her fiercely.

Luckily my cleaning lady was in when the knock came. I gave her instructions to tell whoever it was to go the hell away.

I sank in my office chair, trying to decide what my next move was, when Helga came into my office. "Sorry to bother you, but they won't leave."

"They?"

"A Mr. Ryan and Miss Chloe."

What the hell did they want? Well, I knew what Ryan wanted—to gloat. Was that what Chloe wanted too? I knew she was pissed at me, but she'd never seemed like the vindictive type.

They walked in hand-in-hand. What a fucking sweet little package they made, I thought bitterly. "Ah, there he is. The man who stole part of my company." I scrubbed a hand over my face, knowing I looked like shit.

Chloe smiled at Ryan and he took a step forward. "Hugh—"

I held up a hand to stop him. "Are you here to ruin me completely? It's bad enough you bought half of my company, but now you're here to tell me you've won? That you've gotten her pregnant and are taking all of Grandfather's wealth?"

The guy was a good actor, as he paled slightly. "It's not what you think."

I huffed. "So she is pregnant with the next heir to our family's fortune?"

"Yes, but—"

My laugh was a bitter pill I was forced to swallow. "It doesn't matter. Money means nothing without her," I muttered more to myself.

Seeing them both left me haunted by the memory of Molly, who should have received my letter by now.

"Cousin, Chloe is pregnant, but I've decided not to fight for the money. I won't tell the lawyers anything. And the money is yours if you can produce an heir," Ryan finished.

"Very magnanimous of you, cousin." I rolled my eyes, done with him, and faced Chloe. "You were the best employee I had. Losing you and my company is worse than I thought possible," I admitted. Something I should have said before she'd felt the need to resign.

"You haven't lost her," Ryan said.

My eyes narrowed. I knew I wouldn't like what was said next.

"I'm your partner now," Chloe said with a tentative grin.

Though I loved Chloe as an employee, I wasn't ready to lose my company to her. "You gave her my company? And I've lost everything that matters."

Ryan held up a hand, as if that would make everything better. "Isn't she a better partner than your ex? You just said she was the best thing about your company. With her, you'll have someone who wants to make a difference. It's not like you're losing anything except your ex meddling with your company. You've gained something far more."

Though what he said made sense, I'd never seen my ex as my partner forever. I'd been trying to buy back my shares for a while now.

Chloe stepped forward. "I'd be willing to sell it back to you if you don't want me. I don't want bad blood between us. You will be a cousin... let's just call you an uncle to our child."

I glanced between them. "You'd sell me your half?" I asked, calmer now.

She nodded. "I want you at our wedding."

Holy shit. "You're getting married?" I looked to both of them, waiting for an answer.

"Yes, and I want you there. We don't have much family left. I want us to mend fences. You used to be like a brother to me," Ryan said.

Ryan had still won. I stared at Chloe's flat stomach a second, wondering if Molly was pregnant. If she was, would she tell me?

"Hold onto her, cousin. You don't want to know what it feels like to lose the only woman you've ever loved," I said, rubbing at the ache Molly's absence had left in my chest. I turned to Chloe. "I regret so much. I poured all the work onto you because I knew you would get it done. Maybe you are what this company needs. At least now I'll share it with family."

Chloe came over and wrapped me in a hug. I held on because I'd felt lost and alone. Without my parents and grandparents, I'd had no one. Molly had been that lifeline for me. Though I wanted her, I kissed the top of Chloe's head. She was a good woman and Ryan was a lucky bastard.

I reluctantly let her go, seeing Ryan's jaw flex. "A wedding, huh?" I asked again. They nodded. "I'll be there. And Chloe, I expect to see you at work tomorrow. We have a lot to do."

With my absence at work, and without Chloe there to

keep things going, who knew if we were on track for our next publication?

She grinned and Ryan clasped my hands. "I hope you find someone. It's the best thing that's happened to me."

Then an idea formed. "About that, I have a favor to ask."

THIRTEEN

Molly

The last weeks had been miserable. I'd alternated between crying and sobbing. Work had been awful as I'd been reminded daily of what Hugh had done.

The best news, however, came from Mr. McNeill when he emailed me to tell me that Dad had been granted an appeal. It wouldn't take place for at least a month because it had to be placed on the docket, but that was the only thing that had made me smile in days.

"Wow, it's about time I see that frown disappear."

I glanced up from the computer to see Joe standing there. "Oh, hey."

"What's been up with you lately? I've been afraid to approach you."

"Nothing."

"Come on, Molly. I know you much better than that."

"Okay, man troubles."

Joe gave me an odd look. "What do you mean?"

"Nothing, other than I got into it with the guy I was seeing."

"Oh? Over what?"

"Jeez, you're nosy."

He held up his hands. "Sorry, didn't mean to pry."

"Hey, have you talked to Chloe lately?"

"No. She's your friend. I never talk to her unless you're around. Did something happen?"

I shrugged. "I don't think so. I just was wondering."

He walked away, but our conversation nagged at me for the way he was so curious. I let it drop and went back to the email from Mr. McNeill. That got me thinking about Hugh. I needed to talk to someone, namely Chloe, about things. I'd have to come clean with her about our relationship. Maybe we'd still be friends after she found out, but right now I really needed a shoulder to cry on.

That night I called and texted her but didn't get a response. I wished she'd answer because I needed a sounding board. The phone rang and I jumped. Then a long sigh escaped past my lips as I saw it was Chloe calling me back. "Oh, Chloe, thank God. I need to talk to you."

"I need to talk to you too."

My stomach rolled with the worst wave of nausea. I never got sick like this. I hadn't eaten lunch so it couldn't be food poisoning. "Chloe, I gotta go. I'll call you right back." I made it to the bathroom just in time. Throwing up was one of those things I'd bargain with the devil over. What the hell had happened? I didn't have a fever or headache so it couldn't be a virus. Then it slammed into me like a tank. "Oh, no. Not now. Why now?"

"Hey, are you okay?" someone asked from the stall next door.

"Yeah, sorry. Must've been something I ate."

"Oh, I hate that. Hope you feel better." Then she was gone.

I wiped my mouth and then rinsed it out. How long had it been since my period? Was I due now? I couldn't even think straight for the nausea and turmoil in my head.

I left the office early and picked up a pregnancy test on the way home. Then I did the deed. As I waited for the results, I knew in my heart what it would be. Sure enough, I was pregnant. This was a time I was supposed to be ecstatic. Instead, my heart was heavy with sadness. What should I do? I had to tell Hugh. I knew he'd be happy about the baby, but what about me? Would he still want me?

My phone rang and it was Chloe. Shit, I'd forgotten to return her call.

"Molly! What the hell is going on? You never called me back."

"I'm sorry. Something happened."

"I'm coming over." The call ended.

In some ways, I needed her more than ever, but in others, I dreaded the news I had to share.

The pounding on the door matched the pounding in my head. I turned the knob and Chloe pushed her way in. Then she hugged me. "What's going on?"

"I'm not sure where to begin."

"Try the beginning." She grabbed my hand and drew me to the couch.

"Fine." I took a deep breath and plunged in. "Please don't hate me, but Hugh Hampton and I are a thing."

Her hand sailed through the air. "I figured that after catching the two of you together and it's one of the reasons I'm here."

"You don't hate me?"

"Of course not. I could never hate you. At first I was

pissed that you hadn't told me. That day I came over I was desperate to talk to you, but when I found Hugh there, I got angry. Anyway, all that's old news." She laughed. A little at first, but then harder. "You won't believe this, but the guy I left with, Ryan, is his cousin."

"What!"

"Yeah, we're dating. It's such a small world, isn't it? I can't believe we met them both the night at the party."

"Seriously? The guy you texted me the pic of?"

"Yes, That's who I disappeared with."

"Oh, my God! I can't believe it!"

She aimed her finger at me. "And you and Hugh. Mr. Crabbypants. If he fucks things up, I'm going to kick his ass. He explained everything and I got it."

I scrunched up my face. "He's not crabby with me. Well, he wasn't until... oh, God, I screwed things up something fierce. But, Chloe, there's something else."

"What?"

"I, er, I'm pregnant. And now I don't know what to do."

"I do. You're going to have a baby. What else?" Chloe asked. I was quiet for a second too long. "Don't even tell me you're thinking of getting rid of it."

"No! I would never. It's just that... oh, never mind."

"Tell me."

It wasn't just that she wouldn't believe me, but what kind of person would she think I was? "It's too complicated. And now it's worse since I screwed things up and got pissed off."

"Well, you have to tell him about the baby. He deserves that, at least."

She was right. But the question was how?

Later that week, I got the biggest surprise when Chloe called to tell me she and Ryan were getting married. They had decided to tie the knot since they were in love. I was very excited for my friend, but couldn't help feeling sorry for myself.

A Few Weeks Later

"I can't believe this is happening," I said.

"Me either. I know it's fast but Ryan didn't want to wait," Chloe said. "I'm just so glad you agreed to be my maid of honor."

I fanned my face. "You are so going to make me cry. I'm glad you forgave me for what happened."

She waved the matter away. "It's water under the bridge. I get it now. You found love in the most unexpected place and he's not that bad."

I turned away and wiped at my eyes.

"What is it?" she asked. "You haven't talked to him yet, have you?"

I shook my head. "This is your day. We can talk about my problems another time."

Chloe smoothed her dress and approached me. Her brand-new custom gown had a vintage style. The ivory floral lace form-fitting dress with an extended sweeping train made her look like a princess.

"You're going to make me cry and mess up my makeup if you don't tell me what's going on."

I sat there glumly in the simple blush-pink V-neck dress I'd picked out. "I don't want to see Hugh today, but I have no choice. He's Ryan's cousin. My only solace is I'll be walking with Ian down the aisle."

Her brow arched. “You and Hugh seemed fine at our small pre-wedding dinner. What happened or was that an act?”

I shook my head. “Don’t worry about me. I’ll tell you the sordid details when you get back from your honeymoon. Hugh’s not the man I thought he was.”

Mrs. Landon opened the door. “Honey, it’s time.”

Chloe nodded, but before getting up, she hugged me. “Are you sure you don’t want to give him a chance?”

I shook my head. “I know you two are partners now and that’s great. But if I saw the man a million days from now, it would be too soon.”

Our conversation ended as her mom hovered, waiting.

“We will talk about this tomorrow. Our plane doesn’t leave until the afternoon. There is no way I can wait two weeks to hear what happened.”

I gave her a small smile. “Sure.” My grin widened for her benefit. “Now let’s go get you married.”

We stood and got in our places at the grand church. It was packed with their friends, family and business associates. It was almost overwhelming. Marrying a powerful man came with a few drawbacks.

I walked down the aisle and watched Chloe make her procession. She gazed at Ryan, who was glorious in a classic tux, with a starry look in her eyes. The man was *GQ*-worthy, but he only had eyes for her.

When she reached the altar, Ryan took her hand and in front of everyone dipped his head and kissed her. I held back the sigh in my body. It was so romantic and in that moment I knew they were made for each other.

“Not yet, son,” the reverend said.

“I’m sorry, I couldn’t wait a second longer,” Ryan said.

"When you find the woman of your dreams, it's hard to wait."

And everything turned out perfect until the reception, when Hugh and I went toe to toe.

Ian and I had been dancing. "Hugh is going to blow a gasket." Ian chuckled.

"Not my problem," I declared, even though my heart ached.

"Is that so?" Ian's brow arched and I had to admit the man was striking. "Does that mean I have a shot?" Ian leaned in and whispered, "Watch out, love. He's coming."

Then I was wrenched out of Ian's arms. "Don't touch her," Hugh warned.

That had gotten the attention of all those around us. I should have walked away, but I saw red. "It's none of your business who I dance with," I sneered.

Hugh got in my face. "It is when you're carrying my child."

He couldn't know that and before I could say anything Chloe jerked me away from Hugh as Ryan pulled him aside.

"Molly, get to talking or I'll kick your ass."

"In that dress?" I quipped.

"Exactly."

I sighed heavily and began my tale of the same night she'd met Ryan. "Hugh is paying me to have his baby. Or was, anyway. Until I screwed things up and got pissed off."

Her head tilted and all of a sudden she burst out laughing. "Holy crap. This is... oh, God. Wait until I tell you." Then she went into this long explanation about the deal she and Ryan had made. Soon I was laughing right along with her.

"Those sneaky men. And to think we both got involved

with them," she said. "Molly, you do realize our babies will be cousins?"

"I always thought of you as a sister and now we'll kind of be related." I threw my arms around her. "But I still haven't solved my Hugh problem. I don't know what to do."

"You have to tell him."

"True. But I'm still angry with him. And what if he doesn't care anymore?"

"Why are you angry?"

My explanation was long and tearful. Chloe knew I had a troubled past but had never been given the complete details about my parents until now.

"Molly, why didn't you ever tell me? You know I would've been there for you."

"Yeah, but it was something I needed to keep to myself."

"From the way I see things, Hugh did you a huge favor and now your dad has a chance of being released."

"Wait, so you're siding with him?"

She wore guilt like a crown. "I guess I am. It's not that I blame you for keeping your father's issue a secret and not telling anyone, but you can't blame that part on Hugh. He didn't know. Think about it. He was only trying to help you by using his connections."

Chloe had a valid point. Was I being too hard-headed and ridiculous? Maybe. I'd kept this secret for so long, it was hard to let go. Perhaps it was time.

My head dipped up and down. "I think you might be right."

A grin tugged at the corner of her mouth. "There's no 'might' about it. All you need to do is kiss and make up."

"He might not want me anymore."

"Then you'll live a wonderful, fulfilling life without him. Just you and your child. But I have a feeling that won't happen. Why don't you go find him and tell him now?"

"I don't think I'm ready. There are too many things going on and my dad's upcoming appeal too. Now I have to figure out how to pay that attorney."

"Understood. But waiting too long isn't fair to Hugh. Think about how you'd feel."

She was right. I left the reception soon after and fell asleep early that night, my heart burdened with too much. When the skies turned gray, I gave up on sleeping and got up. I needed some exercise, so I put on my sneakers and took a walk. Forty-five minutes later, when I was in the parking lot of my condo, the sun was rising over the horizon. A new day and a new beginning. For starters, I needed a doctor's appointment for my baby. And then I had to get some legit work done. The last couple of days had been a bust. The files on my desk were stacked too damn high. Maybe I'd go into the office and get an early start on the week, even though it was Sunday.

Two Weeks Later

It was early morning and I was preparing to face the dreaded Monday. My phone tweeted and I was excited to see it was Chloe. "You're back from your honeymoon! I missed you. Was it amazing?"

"It was. Let's meet for lunch today and I'll tell you all about it."

"Then I'll see you at twelve." She made a reservation and gave me the name of the place.

It was a good thing Chloe didn't care about my appearance because I looked like hell today. Purple half-moons occupied the spaces beneath my eyes and my skin was sallow. Maybe it was because I'd thrown up twice after I got to the office. I needed a remedy for that. Morning sickness was no joke.

The hostess at the restaurant greeted me and I gave her Chloe's name. She pointed me in the direction of our table. As soon as I saw Chloe, she stood, and I hugged her, but then a dark shadow loomed behind us. I glanced up to see the figure of a man standing there. At first I thought it might have been the waiter. But then I realized it was no waiter. It was Hugh. What had Chloe done? Why had she invited him here?

FOURTEEN

Hugh

It was true what they said about pregnant women. Molly had a glow about her, or maybe I was just so damn happy to see her.

"Why is he here?" Her question was quiet and didn't hold rebuke.

I stepped forward to answer. "Hear me out." Chloe looked at her friend as if asking her permission as Molly looked ready to bolt. I jumped in again. "I asked for her help. Don't be mad at her."

Chloe was a pistol too. "No, I knew what I was doing. For the record, she planned to talk to you." Then she aimed her gaze at Molly. "I wouldn't have gone behind your back, but he begged me to do this. And the two of you really do need to talk."

"Fine," Molly said, taking a seat.

"Thanks," I said to Chloe.

She whispered something to her friend. Before leaving,

she said loud enough for me to overhear, "Give him a chance."

Molly didn't respond. Chloe sighed before giving me a tight smile and leaving.

I sat, took my napkin and put it in my lap before finally meeting Molly's eyes. Before I could blurt out the speech I'd prepared in my head, the waiter arrived. "What can I get you to drink?" he asked.

A former version of me might have ordered for the both of us. But Molly had changed me. I held her gaze but didn't answer, letting her order for herself.

"Just water," she said.

"Still or sparkling?" he asked.

"Either—no, sparkling."

He nodded. "And you?"

I could kill for a stiff drink, but I said, "Same."

"Do you need another few minutes for your order?" he asked.

"Yes," I said as Molly said, "No."

The waiter's gaze bounced between us. Most likely he sensed the tension and didn't know what to do. I held onto my patience because Molly was angry, and she didn't yet understand why her anger was misplaced.

"Go ahead," I said to her.

She glared at me but answered, "I'll start with a salad. Then I'll have the lobster bisque, a steak medium."

"I haven't decided yet," I said to the waiter. "Let's start with water and salads for now. Thanks." He nodded gratefully before leaving.

"You got me here. What is it you want to say? And then I can leave." She wasn't making this easy for me.

"I'm sorry," I said simply.

"That's it?" she said, trailing off with a mocking laugh.

"No. I wanted to tell you this at the wedding... Anyway, I shouldn't have intervened without speaking to you first. But it came from a good place, I swear." She opened her mouth, but I kept going. "I reached out to a buddy of mine with no idea you worked for his firm. If I'd known, I would have never done it." I could tell she wanted to cut in, but I held up a hand, determined to finish. "Again, if I'd talked to you first as I should have, we wouldn't be at this point. I ask you forgive me knowing my intentions were good."

When I was done, she said nothing for what felt like a few minutes, and I waited for her verdict.

"You were wrong for not talking to me. Do you know how embarrassing it is to admit your father is a felon?"

"But he was innocent."

"That's not what people think when they hear that. Most who are convicted claim innocence. And the last thing I wanted was for people to look at me differently."

"I can respect that and again, I'm so sorry for revealing your secrets, though unintentionally," I said. "I didn't even give your boss your name." Her lips pursed in disbelief. "I gave him your father's name. Again, if I'd known you'd worked there, I wouldn't have done it because I would have known he'd put the pieces together."

Her expression lost some of the fire that had been there. "I wish you'd talked to me first," she said.

"Me too. But I can't go back in time and change things."

She nodded. "There are a lot of things we can't change."

That was ominous. "What do you want to change?"

"Hugh, in the spirit of putting everything on the table, there's something you should know."

I didn't like the look in her eye and especially when she averted her gaze. It couldn't be good news.

"I'll just say it," she said. I waited with air held in my lungs. "I'm pregnant."

I sucked in more air, not expecting that at all. "That's great news." I felt joy and nervousness. I was going to be a father. When she didn't immediately agree, I added, "Isn't it?"

"I don't know." She glanced away again.

The waiter came back with our waters. "Are you ready to order your main course?"

No longer pissed, she gave the waiter a small smile. "I'm sticking with the lobster bisque and a steak medium."

"Well-done," I interrupted. When her eyes froze on mine, I added, "The baby. No bloody or pink steak while you're pregnant."

"How can you know that? Besides, I thought we agreed you weren't going to go all caveman on me and order my food."

"You're right." I shrugged. "Forgive me. I've been reading up on everything and you should be cautious. We can talk about it after." I turned my attention to the waiter. "I'll have the same."

He nodded and walked away.

"Is this how you're going to be? Overbearing?" she asked.

"I just want what's best for you and our child."

She rolled in her bottom lip when it began to tremble. I wanted to pull her in my lap, but we were in public. "Are you really sure about this?" she asked.

Her emotions were everywhere, as were mine. What I wanted was to kiss her and kiss her belly. Instead, I said, "Yes. Honestly, I've never been so sure about anything in my life."

"How can you be? We've only known each other for such a short time."

"I've dated, hooked up with, and met many women in my lifetime. I've never felt like this for anyone until you."

She gave me the side-eye. "You've never had a serious relationship?"

I groaned. "Yes, but even then I knew something wasn't right. I thought things would get better. And they didn't. I should have trusted my gut. I won't make that mistake again. My gut says I shouldn't let you get away. You are the one," I declared.

"But we haven't spoken in weeks. I've been horrible."

"You had legitimate reasons."

"I didn't give you a chance to explain," she said.

"You were hormonal."

Her eyes narrowed. "Are you going to explain away everything or blame things on the pregnancy?"

"Nothing is perfect. But this," I said, waving my finger between the two of us, "is right. So right, I want you to marry me."

FIFTEEN

Molly

Marry him? I gaped for all of a minute.

His stare finally turned into a chuckle. "I'm sorry, Molly. Your expression is priceless."

"You want us to be married?"

"Of course I do. I'm in love with you, if you haven't figured that out yet. I may not be the best at telling you my feelings, or even showing them sometimes, but I want us to be together always. Not just during this pregnancy. You are my world."

I gawked at him. If my eyes hadn't been attached, they would have rolled out of my head. "I-I don't know what to say."

"There's only one word that's needed here. It starts with a Y. Please say yes."

Our gazes merged and so many thoughts tumbled through my head. "Will you let me stand on my own two feet and think for myself?"

"Every day."

"Will you let me make my own decisions without butting in?"

"Absolutely."

"Will you consult with me if you feel the need to do something on my behalf?"

"One hundred percent I will."

"Can we agree to discuss things before any major decisions are made?"

"Indeed we can."

"Then, Mr. Hampton, I will think about it."

His brows shot up. "After all that you're only going to think about it?"

"I'm going to give it some of my most serious thought."

"Then in the meantime, will you be opposed to some physical persuasion?"

"That might be arranged."

After lunch, he took me up to the penthouse and did his best to persuade. The little devil was wicked. He bared his horns and used every trick in the book until he had me begging for mercy.

"Don't stop." My breath wheezed out of me. "Yesss. Right there." The man knew exactly what he was doing. "Ohhh, yes." My belly clenched as I was going to climax.

Then he pulled his mouth off of my mound and with a roguish grin asked, "Will you marry me?"

"Yes! I'll marry you! Just put that tongue of yours back down there."

"And where would that be?"

I opened my eyes to stare open-mouthed at him. Hugh was never this playful, so I had to witness this side of him for myself. "Okay, who are you and what did you do with Hugh Hampton? Because he rarely smiles."

He threw his head back and laughed.

"Oh, my God. Has your body been invaded by an alien?" I got to my knees and examined his face. "No, you look like the real Hugh. Tell me what's going on."

My suspicions must have sunk in. He still chuckled but said, "I'm happy. The happiest man in the world."

"Fine, but I'm the most frustrated woman in the world. You stole my orgasm away and I want it back." My lower lip poked out.

He slid his finger over it. "Don't worry, I'll make it up to you a thousandfold. Every night of our marriage."

"What did you just say?"

"We're getting married. Remember?"

Shit. I had agreed to that, hadn't I? "Right. But you tricked me with that magic tongue of yours. I was tongue-drunk. No fair."

"Babe, everything is fair in love and sex."

"Hugh, it's love and war."

Large hands cupped my cheeks. "My darling Molly, there will never be any wars between us."

"How do you know that? Do you have a crystal ball?"

"No, but I have a large cock that will fuck you mercilessly if you ever think about going to war with me."

"Hmm. I kinda like the sound of that." I giggled as an image of Hugh in a medieval suit of armor came to mind.

"What's so funny?"

"I envisioned you as Sir Hugh, the knight."

"Remember, if I'm a knight, you're wearing a chastity belt."

"Speaking of, I feel like I'm wearing one right now."

"Pretty sure I can remedy that." His brows waggled right before he took a dive into the land of Molly's mound.

There was nothing like Hugh going down on me, except

for his cock. And I was lucky enough to be the receiver of that after he gifted me with not one, but two glorious orgasms. Then he plunged inside of me and rode me to the stars. Sweat beaded both of our bodies after we finished, and I lay panting for oxygen on the sheets.

His nibbles on my breasts brought me back to life. "Ohh, I'm so sensitive. Must be the pregnancy."

"I can't wait to see your belly get round." He rested his palm over my abdomen.

"I'll be honest, that part I am not looking forward to."

Raising himself on one elbow, he asked, "Why not?"

"I don't want to get all fat."

"You won't be fat. You'll be pregnant and beautiful. You're already glowing."

I scoffed. "It was the sex, silly." I brushed his hair off his forehead.

"Let's make a wager. I say you will remain perfect and after the baby comes, you'll be exactly as you are now."

"What are the stakes?"

"Your choice."

"If I win, I'd like my mother moved to a skilled facility closer to here."

He tipped my chin up and kissed me. "It's already in the works. I have someone investigating the best places for her so she can be moved as quickly as possible. You won't have to spend all that time driving to visit her, so you can do it more often if you like."

"Hugh! Are you serious?"

"Of course I am. This is important, Molly. She should be close to you."

I threw my arms around him. "'Thank you' seems so inadequate. I wasn't expecting this until after the baby came."

"I'd love to see it happen in the next week or so."

"I don't deserve you."

"I disagree. I'm the one who doesn't deserve you. So, the wager."

"Hmm. How about a weekend away?"

"You mean you'd leave the baby?"

"No! Forget that." I could never leave my baby. I was already getting warm fuzzies just thinking about holding her.

"Why the smile?"

"Oh, Hugh, I can't wait to hold her."

"What if she's a he?"

"As long as the baby's healthy, I don't care about the sex."

His lips softly touched mine. "How about this? If I win, you cook me dinner for a week and if you win I cook you dinner for a week."

"I like that, but we may have to wait a few weeks after the baby comes because I'm not sure I'll be worth a damn right away."

"My darling, you don't have to worry about that. We can hire a nanny to help you."

"But I want to do it."

"I want you to, but I also want you to enjoy our new son or daughter and you won't if you don't get any sleep."

Wow, I hadn't thought of that. He was so considerate. "How do you manage to think of everything?"

"It's called the internet. I did a bit of research."

"Glad you did, because I haven't done any yet." He was miles ahead of me.

"One other thing. We need to plan a wedding."

"Oh. About that. I don't really want one."

His jaw dropped open. "But Molly, we have to have a

wedding. With my family and business associates, it demands we have one."

"Hugh, I can't. My father can't walk me down the aisle, and Mom can't be there as she is, and I don't have anyone else. So, no, a wedding with a reception is out."

"Molly, please reconsider. It's important for me."

"Hugh, you have to see my side too."

"Then we are at an impasse," he said, his mouth pressing into a thin line.

EPILOGUE

Between Chloe and I, we got Molly to agree to a small wedding. I won her over by explaining how important it was for me to have photos of us on our wedding day that weren't in front of a courthouse. I also added I didn't want our kids to ever think it was a shotgun wedding.

She relented and we picked the place that accommodated what we wanted. She agreed to our special day including her and me. Our only guests would be Chloe and Ryan. Though I could tell she was getting in the spirit of things after shopping for a wedding dress.

"You're going to love it," she said that day.

I followed it up by telling her I'd be happy if she married me naked, except for the fact Ryan would be there as well as the officiator.

Chloe got her to pick wedding colors and asked what Molly thought were fictitious questions about what food she'd serve if we had a big reception to help her get more excited about our tiny wedding.

On the day of, Molly insisted we share a room to get

dressed. She thought it was silly to surprise me. "I know you really want this, but it seems too expensive," she said.

I kissed her cheek and said, "It will be worth it. You'll have pictures to show your mother."

That had been the wrong thing to say. My hormonal wife-to-be began to cry. "I'm sorry. I just wish she could be here."

"I know." I hugged her to me and kissed her temple. I had my tux on, but she still stood in sexy lingerie I had to ignore so I wouldn't fuck her all over the room. "Let me get Chloe to help with your makeup."

"What? You think I'm ugly now?"

She had no idea. "Hell, no. You are the most beautiful woman in the world."

As I held her sobbing, I texted Chloe. When she came, I made excuses to leave.

Then I went into the room and marveled at all my preparations. Molly had to love it or I'd completely fucked this up.

Molly

"Oh, Chloe, it's my wedding day and neither of my parents are here," I cried, uncaring of the mess my makeup was becoming.

"I know, sweetie," she said, patting my back.

"I just feel like leaving. I know Hugh wanted something bigger than a courthouse, but it's killing me."

She pulled back and looked at my face. "Do you want to leave?"

I nodded my head. "I do. But I can't do that to him. He's being so sweet when he wanted a big wedding so the world would know."

"Some men," Chloe teased. I giggled some. It was odd that a man wanted the big wedding. I could say it was a good sign of how much he loved me.

"Let's get you into that dress and then fix your makeup," Chloe urged.

We did just that and as I stood in front of the mirror, I didn't feel the joy I should on my wedding day. I'd dreamed of the big wedding. The only reason I hadn't wanted one was that it felt wrong without my parents.

There was a knock on the door. The fancy place we'd settled on had a wedding planner, which also seemed like a wasted expense. The woman popped her head in and announced it was time.

"Thank you for walking me down the aisle," I said to Chloe on a choked sob after the woman left.

"Always."

We walked out into the foyer in front of the grand double doors. Once we got into position, Chloe said, "Wait here a second. I need to grab you some tissues."

I nodded and sniffed as I thought about walking down an aisle of empty rows. I had a feeling my makeup wouldn't survive my vows as I couldn't stop crying.

"A little birdie told me you needed a tissue."

A lump caught in my throat as I spun. "Dad?" I'd never seen my father looking so handsome, wearing a black tux, and he seemed to glow. It reminded me of when I was a little girl and I thought he was the greatest man on Earth. He held open his arms and I flung myself into them. "How are you here?"

"Hugh."

My makeup was surely ruined for now as I cried like a newborn baby. Then Chloe was there, makeup ready.

When the music started, the fancy double doors opened and beyond them the room was filled with family and friends.

"I'm going to kill and kiss him at the same time," I said.

Dad whispered in my ear as Ryan appeared and took Chloe's arm as they walked down the aisle. "Don't cry, baby. Your mother will worry."

"Wait. Is she here too?"

"Yes."

"Hugh?" I asked.

"He's a good man. I couldn't have picked anyone better for you."

Hugh

Molly had been right about the dress. Seeing her in it made it tough not to throw her over my shoulder and skip to the honeymoon part. But it was seeing the joy on her face as her parents were there for her on this special day that put the grandest smile on my face.

It hadn't been easy. Finding a judge to grant her father an early release while he was on appeal had been tough. I'd been afraid we wouldn't pull it off.

In the end, it had happened. I'd paid a private nurse so her mother could be here too with all her special needs. They were both present and that was the best gift I could give my wife compared with the one she would give to me in the months ahead.

When my son was born, months later, he came into the world on the same day his cousin arrived. Grandfather's lawyers had a tough time not splitting the money between us as we argued against going by the time stamp.

My future with Molly was bright and, funny enough, I had my grandfather to thank for it. If not for the codicil in his will, who knew if I would ever have taken the time with any woman to fall in love?

When I looked at my wife holding our son, I knew I was the luckiest man in the world.

"You know I love you, right?" I told her.

"Only if you know I love you more," she said back.

"Not possible." Then I flashed her another smirk. "How long do we have to wait before I can fuck the hell out of you?"

"A month or so, why? Horny?"

"Always. But I thought why wait? We should start working on baby number two."

When she gaped at me, I took advantage and claimed her mouth. For now, it would do. I showed her exactly how horny I was.

Babies wouldn't remember things like this, would they? Our son was nestled between us during our soul-searing kiss.

THE END

Thank you so much for taking the time to read our Cocky Billionaires Duet. If you could be so kind as to leave a review—just a few words are fine—we would greatly appreciate it.

If you haven't already, read Ryan & Chloe's story in **Dirty Savage Boss**

You may also enjoy the following:

Worth Every Risk

Andi

He was my best friend since we were little. Even though he was off limits, as we grew up, he became my forever, my everything. But I couldn't let my selfish dreams hold him back. They say that if you love someone, you should let them go. I did. He became the world's greatest soccer player. Money. Fame. Beautiful women. He had it all. One thing I never expected was for him to walk back into my life again.

Chase

She was perfect for me in every way. Once we kissed that first time, there was no turning back. But I made a mistake by letting her go. My need for her has only grown. After three long years, I've decided to get her back. Only I'm too late. Someone has taken my place. I don't know if I still love her or if I should hate her. One thing is certain. She is and always has been mine.

Worth Every Risk is a full-length standalone novel.

OTHER BOOKS BY A.M. HARGROVE & TERRI E. LAINE

Cruel & Beautiful standalone series

Cruel and Beautiful

A Mess of A Man

One Wrong Choice

Wilde Players standalone series

Sidelined

Fastball

Hooked

Worth Every Risk

Cocky Billionaire Boss duet

Dirty Savage Boss

Dirty Arrogant Boss

Standalone

A Beautiful Sin

STALK TERRI E. LAINE

Terri E. Laine, USA Today bestselling author, left a lucrative career as a CPA to pursue her love for writing. Outside of her roles as a wife and mother of three, she's always been a dreamer and as such became an avid reader at a young age.

Many years later, she got a crazy idea to write a novel and set out to try to publish it. With over a dozen titles published under various pen names, the rest is history. Her journey has been a blessing, and a dream realized. She looks forward to many more memories to come.

STALK ME AT

Website: terrielaine.com
Facebook: terrielainebooks
Facebook Page: TerriELaineAuthor
Twitter: @TerriLaineBooks
Instagram @terrielaineauthor
Goodreads: terri e laine
Newsletter Signup: click here

Join my fan group
Terri's Butterflies or Terri's Bad Girls Group on Facebook.

I have several upcoming releases, make sure to sign up for my newsletter or check my website for details.

www.terrielaine.com

ALSO BY TERRI E. LAINE

other books authored

by Terri E. Laine

King Maker Trilogy

Money Man

Queen of Men

King Maker

Kingdom Come Duet

Kingdom Come

Kingdom Fall

King Me Duet

King Me

Queen Her

All the Kings Sons Standalone Spinoffs

Arrogant Savior

Rook to Ruin

Bishop to King

Pawn to Knight

King Me Duet

King Me

Queen Her

Him standalone series

Because Of Him

Captivated by Him

Chasing Butterflies standalone series

Chasing Butterflies

Catching Fireflies

Changing Hearts

Craving Dragonflies

Songs for Cricket

Blinded by You Duet

Honey

Sugar

Married in Vegas standalone series

Married in Vegas: In His Arms

Absolutely Mine

Other standalone books

Ride or Die

Thirty-Five and Single

Perfect Night

Unforgettable

other books co-authored

by Terri E. Laine

Cruel and Beautiful

A Mess of A Man

One Wrong Choice

Sidelined

Fastball

Hooked

Worth Every Risk

A Beautiful Sin

Dirty Savage Boss

Dirty Arrogant Boss

A.M. HARGROVE

Reader, Writer, Dark Chocolate Lover, Ice Cream Worshipper, Coffee Drinker, Lover of Grey Goose (and an extra dirty martini), Puppy Lover, and if you're ever around me for more than five minutes, you'll find out I'm a talker.

A.M. Hargrove divides her time between the mountains of North Carolina and the upstate of South Carolina where she pursues her dream career of writing. If she could change anything in the world, she would make chocolate and ice cream a part of the USDA food groups. Annie writes romance in several genres, including adult, new adult, and young adult. Her books usually include lots of suspense and thrills and she sometimes ventures into the paranormal, sci-fi and fantasy blend.

STALK A.M. HARGROVE

If you would like to hear more about what's going on in my world, please subscribe to my mailing list on my website at http://amhargrove.com/mailing-list/.
You can also join my private group—Hargrove's Hangout—on Facebook if you're up to some shenanigans!
Please stalk me. I'll love you forever if you do. Seriously.

www.amhargrove.com
Twitter @amhargrove1
www.facebook.com/amhargroveauthor
www.facebook.com/anne.m.hargrove
www.goodreads.com/amhargrove1
Instagram: amhargroveauthor
Pinterest: amhargrove1
annie@amhargrove.com

For Other Books by A.M. Hargrove visit www.amhargrove.com

For Other Books by A.M. Hargrove visit

https://amhargrove.com/book/
Or
https://readerlinks.com/mybooks/1842

If you would like to purchase signed books, you can do so here: https://amhargrove.com/shop/

Adult Novels

Adult Novels

For The Love Series
For The Love of English
For The Love of Easton
For The Love of My Sexy Geek

Mason Creek Series
Perfect Love (Mason Creek #3)

The Kent Brothers Novels
ACER
RAIDEN
CRUZE (TBD)

The West Sisters Stand Alone Novels:
One Indecent Night
One Shameless Night
One Blissful Night

The West Brothers Stand Alone Novels:
From Ashes to Flames
From Ice to Flames

From Smoke to Flames

Stand Alones
Secret Nights
I'll Be Waiting

The Men of Crestview Stand Alone Novels:
A Special Obsession
Chasing Vivi
Craving Midnight

The Edge Series Stand Alone Novels:
Edge of Disaster
Shattered Edge
Kissing Fire

The Tragic Duet Stand Alone Novels:
Tragically Flawed, Tragic 1
Tragic Desires, Tragic 2

The Hart Brothers Series:
Freeing Her, Book 1
Freeing Him, Book 2
Kestrel, Book 3
The Fall and Rise of Kade Hart
The Hart Brothers Series Boxset
Sabin, A Seven Novel
A Hart Brothers Novel Spin-off

YA/NA Clean Romance
The Guardians of Vesturon Series:
Survival

Resurrection
Determinant
reEmergent

Co-Authored Books

Cruel & Beautiful:
Cruel and Beautiful
A Mess of a Man
One Wrong Choice

A Beautiful Sin

The Wilde Players Dirty Romance Series:
Sidelined
Fastball
Hooked

Worth Every Risk—
A Wilde Players Spin-Off

www.ingramcontent.com/pod-product-compliance
Lightning Source LLC
LaVergne TN
LVHW012116170826
845678LV00014BA/2965

9798461833732